K would ride tomorrow...

Sixty-two officers and men who had lived the same lives, drunk the same harsh whiskey in Hagar's bars, and might—some of them—die together at the hands of the Sioux.

> **Trooper Paul Fraley** . . . *going into his first major battle at nineteen, wondering whether he'd ever get back to that girl in Suds Row.*

> **Sergeant Jim Bestwood** . . . *the cavalry had been his life for twenty years. There was no going back now, even if he wanted to.*

> **Captain Frank Garland** . . . *who would lead his men tomorrow into the Dakota badlands to rescue the son of Washington's land-greedy Senator Mark Hardin—not because of political pressure; not because Lieutenant Hardin had been a good officer; but because the lieutenant had been a member of Company K. And K took care of its own . . .*

William Chamberlain, known to millions for his stories of army action in *The Saturday Evening Post*, is at his best in this exciting novel of a desperate rescue mission into the land of the deadly Sioux.

TRUMPETS OF COMPANY K

William Chamberlain

BALLANTINE BOOKS • NEW YORK

For MARIAN
*An Army wife, without whose
help and encouragement this book would
not have been written.*

Library of Congress Catalog Card Number: 54-7561

ISBN 0-345-30551-5

Printed in Canada

First Edition: May 1954
Fourth Printing: June 1982

1. The Empty Land

THE TRAIN, chuffing up out of the prairie's eastern rim, poured a great cloud of black smoke from its squat, barrel-like stack and the haze hung darkly above the dun ground in the last of the day's sunlight. The heat of the afternoon still lingered but already there was a hint of winter in the little wind gusts which came out of nowhere to stir the yellow dust in Hagar's main street and play captiously with the tumbleweeds at the town's edge. For this was a new and raw town which had sprung up overnight, almost, when the rails had stopped here—a rude and lusty and brawling town, flaunting herself shamelessly.

A man's town, peopled by men who drifted restlessly through this new land, seeking new things or trying to forget old. Range riders who stalked along Hagar's one and unnamed street, their heels scraping on the boards of the tilted sidewalks and with their spurs jingling faint music; agency Indians, blanketed and sullen with the knowledge of new hunting grounds which had been snatched away from them; railroad men waiting impatiently for the time when the rails would start to move westward again; soldiers from Fort Duncan, two miles away on the low bluffs above Cache Creek, in the direction of the sunset. A man's town.

Frank Garland moved impatiently along the one street, pushing his way through the little knot of loafers in front of the Deerfoot saloon and indifferent to the angry stares which followed him as he passed. He came presently to the depot—a wooden box of a building hunched on its platform. Here he halted, waiting for the train to come in.

Winter would come early this year, he thought. The prospect depressed him a little for winter was a time of

1

inactivity in this land and inactivity was a thing that he feared. He was a man pushed hard by memories and those memories could best be kept in check when he was riding with a horse between his knees and Company K strung out in a thin column behind him and the long trail stretching ahead.

There was a certain peace that came to him then. A peace in the muted jangle of cavalry equipment slamming against McClellan saddles; a faint serenity in the snort of horses, and the rough banter of troopers, in the taciturnity of Jim Bestwood, his first sergeant, and in the quiet understanding of Oglethorpe Henderson who rode with him, second in command. Even at night a man could forget his bitterness a little when he lay with his head pillowed on his saddle and looked straight up into a clear heavens studded with its stars.

Martha still came back to him then, her face framed in the starlight, but somehow the hurt was easier to bear with the muffled and familiar sounds of K around him. It was three years now since she had gone in that abortive raid on Fort Corse. Well, it did a man little good to remember.

Now, he shrugged the thought impatiently away as he saw that the train was entering the edge of town. The stationmaster, a stolid man whose left leg dragged a little from a bullet taken in the peach orchard at Gettysburg, waved at Garland as he went past.

"Expectin' somebody, Frank?" he asked.

Garland nodded absently. "That's right," he said, not amplifying his answer. The stationmaster stopped and wiped at his face with a red bandanna.

"Hot as hell," he grunted. "Too hot for this time of year. Liable to blow up a blizzard. I've seen that happen before."

Garland said nothing to that and the stationmaster went on toward the platform's edge, gimping as he went. The man's question had irritated him a little—he didn't exactly know why. He had little interest in the woman who was arriving on the train. She was Gil Hardin's fiancée, coming out from Boston or Baltimore or New York—shadowy places in the east which he no longer wished to remember —to marry Gil. A man out here on the frontier had no business to marry, Garland thought. He had found that out. Still, it was no business of his even though Gil Hardin had now been assigned as an extra lieutenant in Company K.

And now this girl was coming on the train and Gil was still out on a scout with two squads of K and the business of meeting her had fallen to him. In spite of himself, a little thread of worry ran through Garland's mind. Those two squads with Gil should have been back by sundown yesterday. It was not good when a scout did not return by the appointed time; not this summer, it wasn't.

There were rumors of a new land steal being engineered in Washington—one which would dig deeper into the treaty lands of the Sioux—and uneasiness hung in the air out here. Two weeks ago, Broken Feather had led his band from the reservation—drifting silently back into the badlands to the northwest, taking his women and children with him. Other bands would follow if something wasn't done soon. It was a scant three years now since this country had boiled with war as Custer and the Seventh had ridden out of Fort Lincoln to meet destiny on the banks of the Little Big Horn. That could happen again, Garland was thinking soberly—it would take only a spark to start an uprising. And there was only Fort Duncan here, with its four companies of cavalry, to stop it should it come.

The train's whistle cut short his thoughts as it came chuffing in, fresh smoke pouring from its stack. He wondered a little what Gil's fiancée would look like. Pretty and petted and spoiled, he guessed. He had seen other girls who had come out here from Boston or New York or Baltimore.

Janet Davenport sat on the coach's hard seat, looking out of the grimed window as the jolting train approached the town called Hagar. A lone shanty appeared on the prairie first, its warped boards graying in the last of the sun and its shadow stretched out lonesomely as though

3

yearning for the oncoming train. Janet shivered a little—recoiling involuntarily from the stark lonesomeness of this vast and empty land. The feeling had been growing steadily in her ever since they had entered Dakota Territory. Suddenly she desperately wanted the comfort of Gil's arms about her; wanted to hear the reassurance of his voice.

Then the conductor came through the train calling, "Hagar! End of the line. Hagar!" and the crude sheds and the corrals and the more solid houses of the town began to march past her window as she waited and watched.

There was a long, wide street out there deep in dust and with the false fronts and the wooden canopies of its buildings lending a false air of permanence to the place. But, Janet sensed with a clear perception, there was no permanence. Once the railhead had gone, this town would go, too. For there was nothing here to sustain it except the specious and brawling life which the railhead had brought and that was not enough. Hagar would melt back into the waterless earth and nothing would be left except the ghosts of houses falling down and the twin ribbons of rails fading over the horizon to the west.

The train ground to a jerky stop and she sat quietly for a moment, biting at her lower lip and looking thoughtfully through the smeared window. People bustled about her, hauling packages and valises from beneath seats and crowding down the narrow aisle. She paid no attention, straining her eyes for a glimpse of Gil. Without her willing it, her eyes picked out a man who stood a little apart from the rest and she vaguely wondered who he was while her mind worried over the fact that Gil wasn't there.

It was the calm detachment of the stranger that had attracted her, she thought. He stood with the crowd and yet not of it—a tall, loose-limbed man wearing the uniform of a captain of cavalry and carrying the inevitable sidearm which was the badge of this country. A man perhaps ten years older than Gil but a brother officer, she was sure, and her attention quickened a little as she gave him a closer regard. There was a certain hard purposefulness

4

in the manner in which he moved toward the train now; a sureness in the lines about his mouth and in the hard, flat planes of his face and in the schooled carriage of his shoulders.

He disappeared from her sight momentarily and then she heard a new voice speaking to the conductor at the forward end of the coach.

"Miss Davenport with you, Ed?"

"Yep," the conductor answered. "Been taking good care of her, Frank. Where's Gil?"

"Hasn't got back yet from a scout up the Blackbird," the man named Frank was answering. "I'll see that Miss Davenport gets out to the post."

"Shouldn't think that a man'd want to go sky-hootin' off in the hills when he's got a pretty girl coming out to see him," the conductor answered. "Wasn't that way when I was young, Frank."

"Sometimes a man doesn't have a choice, Ed. Gil should have been back yesterday. Where's Miss Davenport?"

"Down the coach. Just pick the only pretty one."

Janet saw him, then, coming down the aisle toward her and she got slowly to her feet with that faint emptiness beginning to gnaw at her again—then he came to her and stood for a moment, looking down at her from his greater height and not yet speaking. She saw that he was taller than she had thought at first; saw, too, that there were premature patches of gray at his temples (for Frank Garland was not yet thirty-three) and that there were deep lines about his mouth and something faintly shadowed in his eyes.

A sadness, perhaps.

Beautiful, Frank Garland was thinking—but then Gil Hardin would demand beauty in any woman who was to become his wife. That was one of the things that went with Gil's make-up; a part of the man's overweening ego. He was not fond of Gil Hardin, Garland thought suddenly but put the thought away.

He said, his voice revealing nothing at all, "Miss Davenport? I am Captain Frank Garland. I'll take you out to

5

Fort Duncan—Gil has been unavoidably detained, I'm afraid."

"I am happy to meet you, captain." Janet gave him the full benefit of her eyes for the first time. "Gil has spoken of you in his letters."

Garland thought: *There is nothing good that Gil would write in his letters. Not Gil. And Janet Davenport is afraid of something.* No business of his but his mind clung stubbornly to it. *Afraid of Gil? Of this country out here?*

She was saying, then, "I heard you telling the conductor about Gil. It seems strange—I would not have thought that Gil would have allowed anything to interfere with his meeting me here, captain——"

She caught herself then; gave Garland her hand—firm and cool, and Frank felt his mind probing again for that faint something which haunted the back of her eyes. It bothered him a little—he did not wish to be bothered by Gil Hardin; nor by Gil Hardin's fiancée.

He said, "I'm sorry, ma'm. Gil's military duties took him at an unfortunate time. I expect he may be back by the time we get out to the fort."

"It's all right, of course," Janet murmured. "It was kind of you to meet me, captain."

Garland nodded and turned abruptly; gathering her hand luggage together, he led the way out to the coach. Corporal McNair had come, he saw. A light wagon, hitched to a team of bays, had pulled up to the platform's edge and the soldier held the horses steady as Garland loaded Janet's bags. He helped her to the back seat, then settled himself beside her and spoke curtly to the driver.

"Take us to Major Kingman's quarters on the post," he said and was suddenly acutely aware of the faint perfume which came from the girl beside him.

Corporal McNair, a squat and weathered man with the marks of campaigns—against Indians and the bottle— laid deep on him, grunted cheerfully, "Hup, Bess! Sam!" and the wagon lurched heavily out into the dusty street beyond the depot.

They went on down Hagar's single thoroughfare, little

dust bombs exploding yellowly from beneath the feet of the horses as the sun began to dip beneath the horizon, red and vaguely ominous. Garland's mind went back to those two squads which had not yet returned from the scout up the Blackbird and his foreboding of the earlier afternoon returned.

Broken Feather's band was out there somewhere. Perhaps other bands had joined him by now. He had given Gil Hardin orders to avoid a fight—but, damn the man, could you trust him to follow orders when it suited him not to do so? Perhaps he should have sent Oglethorpe Henderson to lead the scout, instead. But he had given Gil Sergeant Brecheen, one of the best of K's noncoms, as second in command. Toronto Peters, too, as civilian scout. And now Gil was overdue. A day overdue.

He was aware, suddenly, that Janet Davenport had turned a little and was looking questioningly at him. "Something is bothering you, captain?" she asked. "Gil, perhaps?"

"He'll be all right," Garland answered her, his voice more brusque than he had meant it to be. He softened it a little as he spoke again. "It was a routine scout, Miss Davenport. There's nothing to worry about."

She was silent again as they went on down the street.

Agency Indians lounged sullenly in front of Mahan's store, dirty blankets wrapped about their shoulders; a half-dozen range ponies switched nervous tails at the flies as they stood—drowsing on three legs—at the hitchrack in front of the two-story hotel. Farther along, the doors of the Deerfoot saloon swung suddenly outwards to spew a man into the dust. He picked himself up awkwardly, stood looking for a moment over his shoulder and then went away, profanely slapping the dirt from his trousers.

Garland's eyes narrowed a little as he recognized the man. Whitewater Charley, a breed who ran Arco Blaine's errands and who did Arco Blaine's bidding. And, if Whitewater Charley was back in Hagar, it meant that Arco would not be far away. Frank Garland's mouth flattened out a little at the thought. He had warned Arco Blaine to stay away; the man was a fool to come back without some compelling reason and Garland had a sudden premonition that that reason was not unconnected with the coming land steal which was in the wind. It would be the sort of thing that attracted men like Arco Blaine.

Garland glanced at Janet out of the corners of his eyes as the surge of the mule skinner's profanity reached out to them. "A rough town, Miss Davenport," he murmured. "A rough country. You must not expect too much."

"I am learning that, captain," she said.

There was a cool flatness in her voice and her face was set rigidly to the front as she drew stiffly away from him; straightened her shoulders. Like, Garland thought with a faint amusement, First Sergeant Jim Bestwood on parade. But it didn't matter. There had been other women who had come out here during the ten years that he had been on the frontier. Some had stayed. Some had gone back. Perhaps most had gone back.

And that thought sent the old familiar pain running through him again. For Martha, who had come out here to him—lips smiling and her eyes unafraid—had been one of those who had stayed until that raid by marauding Sioux had taken her away from him forever at Fort Corse. A chance shot by a drunken Indian and Martha had died while he had been riding with a column a hundred miles to the west. . . .

Janet Davenport stirred beside him. "You are Gil's commanding officer, are you not, captain?" she asked suddenly.

Garland nodded absently. "Yes," he said.

"You sent him out—on this scout?"

Garland frowned a little, not quite knowing where this was leading him. "Yes, I sent him out, Miss Davenport," he said then. "It is routine here. I am afraid that you will find that out when you are Gil's wife."

He turned a little to look at her but her face was still set straight ahead so that he couldn't see her eyes and that bothered him a little. Somehow Janet Davenport had managed to put him in the wrong over something and he didn't know what it was. His irritation deepened.

"It would seem to me that someone else could have gone on that scout—when everyone knew that I was coming." Janet said then with no particular expression in her voice. "Are there not other lieutenants at Fort Duncan, captain? Gil is not the only one?"

Garland saw Corporal McNair's shoulders jerk suddenly as the soldier straightened in his seat. McNair said violently, "Hup, Bess! Step along, you wind-broken dead beat!" and Garland grinned a little; he could picture the outrage which must be on McNair's craggy face as he swung the whip.

For there was a pride which ran in Company K and the thought that a lieutenant of K would want to be excused from leading a scout in order that he might get married was an abhorent and unnatural thing to Corporal McNair's mind. A thing somehow shameful. A thing not to be noised abroad.

The good humor went out of Garland's face. For Gil Hardin had tried to beg off of this scout and Garland had refused him. There had been a stormy meeting in Garland's quarters that night before the column had filed out through Fort Duncan's main gate six days ago.

He remembered it now.

2. "You March at Five Tomorrow"

THE SUN had gone down but the last of the day's heat still lay with a heavy sultriness over Fort Duncan's parade ground as Frank Garland came to his quarters. A single room, Spartanly furnished, but he had it to himself as befitted the senior captain of the garrison. A rude table in the center with its oil lamp and its untidy litter of books and papers. A cot in a corner covered with an army blanket. Deer heads on the walls and boots in a corner and a comfortable chair which the company artificer had made out of willow and rawhide. A man's room.

Home to Frank Garland—now that Martha had gone.

He made himself a drink, using the whiskey to dull the acrid bite of the alkali water, and stood by the window for a moment, listening to the muted clatter which came from the mess halls across the way where the four companies, which formed the garrison of Fort Duncan, were at supper. Yesterday had been the same as this, he thought with a faint dissatisfaction. And tomorrow would be the same and the day after. The monotony ate into a man with the persistence of the slow drip of rain eroding the red hills which stretched away to the northwest.

For nothing changed here at Fort Duncan. There was the baked parade with its flagpole at the far end. And the line of the log barracks with the company stables beyond them. The commissary and the sutler's store and the main guard gate with the sentry on Post No. 1 pacing along his beat. Thirty yards past the gate in either direction; thirty yards back. One-two-three-four; turn and one-two-three-four. Day in and day out. . . .

And this had been his life, Frank Garland reflected dourly, since that day—sixteen years gone now and hazy

10

in his memory—when he had first lifted his hand under the recruiting sergeant's hard stare and had taken the Army's oath and accepted the Army's cloth. That had been back in eighteen hundred and sixty-two, a long time ago. He had been seventeen.

Three years with the Army of the Potomac after that. Second Bull Run, Chancellorsville and Antietam; wounded at Gettysburg and brevet second lieutenant of cavalry after that bitter fight at Yellow Tavern when the war was drawing swiftly to its preordained close. Then garrison duty in New Orleans where the Knights of the White Camellia were growing like poisonous mushrooms; and so on westward to Texas to help counter the threat which the usurper, Maximilian, posed. Finally the frontier here in Dakota Territory. Ten years of it. Long years. . . .

Garland finished his drink; put the tin cup down and lighted the oil lamp against the growing dusk as he heard impatient footsteps come pounding along the baked path which fronted Officers' Row. That would be Lieutenant Gil Hardin, he guessed. He had left word at headquarters that he wanted young Hardin to report to him when the lieutenant came back from town. He suspected that Gil was not going to be pleased when he told him that he was to lead the scout up the Blackbird tomorrow. Well, it didn't matter. The Army was not obliged to please its people.

Then Gil stood in the open doorway, light from the smoky lamp washing across his sharp face, and his shoulders blotting out the twilight which deepened across the parade ground. Garland turned a little, noting without pleasure the flushed, too-handsome face and impatient eyes. An overbearing young man, Frank thought drily— too new in his experience out here and too arrogant with the knowledge that wealth and position lay behind him. For his father, Senator Mark Hardin, was a man who sat in the seats of the mighty in Washington. Like his son, proud and impatient and arrogant with power.

11

Now, Frank Garland said evenly, "Come on in, Gil. Will you have a drink?"

"No, thanks," young Hardin said shortly. "I've got other things to talk about."

"Such as?" Garland asked softly.

Gil Hardin came in, then, making no attempt to conceal the fact that he was angry, and Garland waved him to a seat on the cot at the far side of the room. Gil said roughly, "Look here, Frank, they told me over at the orderly room that you've set me up to lead that scout up the Blackbird tomorrow! You know as well as I do that——"

"That's right, Gil," Garland interrupted. "You'll have two squads—Sergeant Brecheen has the details as to that. I'm sending Toronto Peters along with you. Listen to him and listen to Brecheen—they're old hands out here. They know the country and they know the Indians."

A slow red began to creep up into Gil's face as he started to get to his feet. Garland waved him back. "I'm not through yet, lieutenant," he said drily.

For a moment he thought that Gil Hardin was going to disobey what was more than half a command. Well, if it had to come to a showdown, this was as good a time and place as any to handle it. He took a cigar from a can on the table and set it alight while he turned his head a little to lay his strict attention on Hardin.

"Broken Feather has taken his band into the hills," he said finally, keeping his voice flat and even. "You know that. It may be that he's on the Blackbird. If he is, he is a threat to the security of this post. You will scout up the river for two days—locate the band, if you can. You will be careful to avoid a fight. What we want right now is information and not war. Do you understand?"

"I understand," Gil Hardin said shortly. "I think that I understand too much."

Frank Garland allowed the blue cigar smoke to trickle up past his eyes. "Yes?" he said. "Go on, lieutenant."

The other hunched forward to the edge of the cot, glowering into the lamplight. It touched the blue of his shell jacket, which was too smartly tailored for this land, and glinted on his boots—English leather—and washed across the sulky planes of his narrow face.

He said roughly now, "You've got to send somebody else to lead that scout up the Blackbird. You know well enough, I dare say, that Janet is coming on the train next Tuesday and I'll be damned if I mean to be off in the hills somewhere, chasing a bunch of moth-eaten Agency Indians, when she gets here! Not after the time that I have been waiting for her!"

"My guess is that Broken Feather has got a hundred braves riding with him," Garland said shortly. "And you'll not find them much moth-eaten, Gil. Ideas like that can set your scalp to swinging from a Sioux lodgepole. Today is Thursday. Two days up the Blackbird; two days coming back will put you in Fort Duncan again on Monday night. That gives you plenty of time left in which to meet Miss Davenport, I think."

"And if something goes wrong and I'm late in getting back. What then?"

"I expect you to see that nothing does go wrong," Garland said thinly. "That is the reason that you are an officer, Gil. That is the reason that West Point put those shoulder straps on you. You should know that."

"I don't care for preaching, Garland," Hardin retorted, the edge sharpening in his voice. "You can save that."

Frank Garland paid no attention to that. "Brecheen has orders as to what to take. I'll repeat them to you now. A hundred rounds per man for the carbines. Eighteen for the pistols. Enough grain in the saddlebags for four days. Move up the Blackbird to Benner's Creek, scouting as you go, and be back here at Fort Duncan by Monday night. Is that clear?"

Gil Hardin still sat hunched on the cot, his face dark in the smoky light, and Garland guessed that he hadn't even heard. Then Gil got slowly up; moved around the table so that he was opposite Frank. Then he flung a hand out violently.

"Damn it, Garland," he said, his voice thick with his

anger, "can't you see that this is no time for me to be running off on some wild-goose chase like this? There are other lieutenants here who could take out this confounded detail as well as I can! Stover, Jenks, Henderson! Any one of them!"

"Any one of them could take it out better than you could, Gil," Frank Garland told him quietly. "I know that."

"Then why me?" Hardin demanded.

Garland sat quietly in his chair for a moment, studying his subordinate while he savored his cigar and sweated gently in the heat. "Lieutenant," he said then, the whisper of a lash coming into his voice, "you have led exactly one scout out of this post since April. All of the other lieutenants have led more—a good many more. I do not propose to put your duty off on them again even though Miss Davenport is coming on next Tuesday. Is that quite clear?"

He noted the red flush which crawled slowly up into Gil Hardin's face. Could it be, Garland wondered with a quick feeling of shock, that Gil Hardin was afraid? He put the idea impatiently aside. Gil was just impressed with his own importance, annoyed that he should be made to conform to the routine which governed the others. And he had a young man's impatience to see again the girl that he was going to marry soon. That was all. That had to be all, Frank Garland decided soberly.

For a moment, and against his will, he hesitated a little. Maybe Thorpe Henderson was well enough to go out again this time—let Gil's turn go until later on. Then he remembered the worried look which had come to be a part of Mary Henderson's pinched face and he shook his head.

"You will lead the scout, Gil," he said curtly. "That is an order and not open to any more argument. Have you got any further questions—about your mission?"

Gil Hardin stood there for a moment longer, staring back at Garland while anger flared darkly in his eyes. Then he straightened his heavy shoulders and arrogance was thick in his voice when he spoke.

"I see," he said. "You have chosen to ride me since I

14

have been in this command, Captain Garland." (And that was a lie, Frank Garland thought.) "I resent that. Furthermore, I can assure you that I have friends—in Washington —who will be interested to hear of the Prussian attitude which seems to be popular with the senior officers here at Fort Duncan. And they will hear, captain!"

"You mean that as a threat, lieutenant?" Frank asked softly.

"You can take it any way that you like. The facts will speak for themselves."

"Then let them speak," Garland said shortly. "You will march at five tomorrow morning. Good night, lieutenant."

He sat for a long moment after Gil Hardin had gone, disturbed a little for it gave him no pleasure to lay the whip on another officer. And the threat that Gil had made was not an idle one, he knew, but gave the matter little thought. This was war out here on the frontier and you didn't fight wars from Washington. Not successfully, anyway. He had learned that the hard way when he had marched and fought with the Army of the Potomac.

His cigar was dead again as he picked it up and he turned it slowly in his fingers while he debated the fixing of another drink; decided against it—for he was a man who touched liquor lightly—and lighted the cigar again. Shadows from the smoking lamp huddled in the far corners of the room and, outside, the stars were beginning to come out above the empty parade ground.

This was the time of day that was the hardest—the time that he missed Martha the most. *Damn it, a man had no business to think! Soldiering was enough of a chore without that!* In a moment, he'd wash up; go on down to the mess which the sutler ran for the bachelor officers in the back of his store. Then the inevitable poker game until he was tired enough to tumble into his cot for dreamless sleep. Such things kept a man's mind running in safe channels.

Boots scraped on the walk outside and a man's voice called with a cheerful lift, "Frank, you there?" and Ogle-thorpe Henderson came into the room, the yellow light

15

slanting across his lean face and the saber, slung from his belt, proclaiming him to be the Officer of the Day.

Garland's spirits lifted a little—he was fond of this lanky lieutenant who was acting adjutant at Fort Duncan, while Captain Dubois was on leave, but who habitually rode with K when the company took the field. Frank waved a hand toward the cot. "Sit down, Thorpe. I'm glad you dropped by. I've got the mugwumps this evening, I guess."

Henderson grinned, moving across the room to seat himself on the bed. "Spooks riding you, Frank?" he asked.

"Maybe. Anything special on your mind?"

"Not much," Oglethorpe Henderson said thoughtfully. "I passed Gil Hardin by headquarters. He looked like he's just been bitten by a mad coyote, Frank."

Garland smiled tightly. "He'll probably get over it. I just gave him orders that he would lead the scout up the Blackbird tomorrow. He wasn't happy. Suggested that somebody else should go. Like you, for instance."

Oglethorpe Henderson's face was sober as he sat there, bent forward so that his forearms rested across his knees. Freckles dotted his honest, homely face. Like Frank Garland he had been out here on the frontier for a long time now.

"Maybe I should go, at that, Frank," he said slowly. "A wagon train pulled into Hagar this evening. Reported that they were hit by Indians over near Red Butte. One man killed. Two wounded. It was a small war party and the train was able to fight its way out."

Garland's face turned hard. "Broken Feather's people?" he asked. Henderson shook his head.

"The freighters didn't think so. They said that these Indians looked more like Uncpapas—that would be Dark Buffalo's band, Frank."

"So they're off the reservation, too," Garland murmured. "This thing can get bad, Thorpe. Damned bad."

"You want me to take that scout tomorrow, Frank?"

Garland shook his head tiredly. "It's Gil's turn—a

whole lot past Gil's turn, Thorpe. A man has to learn sometime. He'll take the scout."

Oglethorpe Henderson shrugged. "He's a bad man to have as an enemy, Frank. Mary's folks live in Washington, you know. They are always writing her about Senator Mark Hardin, knowing that Gil is here at Fort Duncan. The senator's a shaggy bear, they say. If you don't watch yourself, he'll have your hide tacked up against the door of his wickiup one of these days."

Garland grinned tightly at that. "I can be a shaggy bear myself, Thorpe, when I have to. A man's worth out here isn't measured by what his father may be in Washington. How sure were those freighters that it was Uncpapas that attacked them?"

"Pretty sure. I've talked with Toronto Peters about it. He thinks that it's a pretty good bet that Dark Buffalo has followed Broken Feather off the reservation."

"The Old Man know?"

"I told him a little while ago," Oglethorpe Henderson said in a sober voice. "He agrees with Toronto's guess. Thinks there may be more behind this than just the usual fuss over the quality of the beef which the agent is issuing."

Garland drew on his cigar; found it dead and dropped it into the can on the table which served as an ash tray. After a moment he got slowly out of his chair to pace up and down the small room, forehead furrowed and mouth set into a faint scowl. Oglethorpe Henderson watched, his own eyes troubled.

"The major's right, Thorpe," Garland said finally. "The Indians wouldn't leave the reservation with winter coming on if they didn't have a good reason. Only, what is that reason? The new land grab that we've been hearing about? It could be that."

"It could be," Henderson agreed sourly. "It's a hell of a thing. Do you know anything specific about it?"

"Rumors, that's all," Garland said shortly. "And you can hear anything in a rumor. If past experience is any guide, though, I'd say that somebody has got his eyes on

17

fresh treaty lands. The question is who and why and where?"

Henderson nodded. "I've got a hunch that Arco Blaine knows the answers to some of those questions. Toronto Peters told me that he saw Arco and Whitewater Charley down at the trading post at Esperance a week ago. That's on the southern edge of the reservation—and Whitewater Charley has been friendly with Broken Feather in the past. Could mean something."

Garland abruptly stopped his pacing, his face dark. "I have warned Arco Blaine to stay out of this country," he said roughly.

Henderson shrugged his shoulders. "I guess maybe he didn't believe you, Frank," he said slowly. "After the court-martial he promised that he'd be back. You remember?"

"I remember," Frank Garland said shortly. "I'm not likely to forget that."

3. Empty Saddles in the Sunset

WELL, that had been six days ago, Frank Garland was thinking now as the light wagon jounced over the rough road to Fort Duncan. And Gil Hardin and his two squads had not yet returned. The depression, which had flogged all day at him, settled more heavily onto his shoulders now.

"There are other lieutenants at Fort Duncan, Miss Davenport," he said finally in answer to Janet's question. "It was Lieutenant Hardin's turn to go. That is all. He'll probably be waiting for you when we get to the post."

She turned to face him squarely now and there was something a little accusing in the directness of her gaze. "That is the only reason that Gil went on this particular patrol, captain?"

"No other reasons," Garland told her curtly. "Should there have been, Miss Davenport?"

She studied him for a long moment, her lower lip caught between her teeth as she held her face toward him. A beautiful woman, Frank Garland thought again. And a woman accustomed to having her own way—even though he still could not fathom what lay behind that shadow in her eyes. Anyway, she would be an ornament to Gil's home—back in Washington someday—for Gil Hardin made no pretense of hiding his ambitions. Nor of letting it be known that there were those—many of them—in the capital who were willing to see that those ambitions were realized.

"I don't know," Janet answered thoughtfully. "I have wondered. You don't like Gil very much, do you, captain?"

How in the devil, Frank Garland wondered angrily, had they gotten off onto a line of conversation such as this? And what possible business did he have in discussing Gil

Hardin with the girl who had come out here to marry him?

He said, picking his words carefully, "I neither like nor dislike Gil, Miss Davenport. I think that we had better let the matter drop, don't you?"

"He hates you," Janet answered gravely. "I could read that in his letters. I wonder why?"

"A man does not have to have a reason to hate," Garland told her drily. "Forget it, ma'am."

Corporal McNair turned his head a little, then, his profile blunt against the sunset. "That's Arco Blaine ridin' towards us, cap'n," he said in a softly cautious voice. "I heard in town that he'd come back to these parts."

Garland nodded curtly and turned his attention to the rider who was approaching. He was glad of the excuse to discontinue the conversation with Janet Davenport—it had gotten onto dangerous grounds. And he had already recognized Arco Blaine.

The rider was a scant hundred yards away, pulling his horse down to a walk and lifting a hand to signal that he wanted to talk to those in the wagon. Garland said, "Pull up, McNair," and waited, his eyes quietly watchful now.

Arco Blaine came on, swinging easily in his saddle, and then pulled the black up beside the wagon, lounging in his saddle as he allowed his eyes to run lazily over Janet Davenport. He was a darkly insolent man with a chiseled face, deeply tanned above the thin line of mustache on his upper lip. A man a little younger than Frank Garland and with a recklessness running through his eyes and the marks of hard living already graved about his mouth. After a long moment, he swung his gaze back to Garland, lips curling in a thin smile.

"Frank," he said, bowing sardonically. "I see that you have pleasant duties this evening. My congratulations." His eyes went boldly back to Janet and she flushed a little beneath his stare.

"I heard that you were back in this country, Arco," Frank Garland said softly. "I warned you once not to do that because this country is not big enough to hold the two of us. I do not intend to warn you again."

20

Arco Blaine eased himself a little in the saddle and laughed shortly under his breath but cold anger had come into his eyes. "You don't change, do you, Frank?" he murmured. "I stopped merely to pass the time of day. Your manners, captain? Do you not intend to make me known to the young lady?"

"That is not necessary," Garland said, clipping his words harshly. "I will be in Hagar tonight, Arco. I will expect to find you gone by then."

Dark blood moved swiftly up into Blaine's face. He said violently, "You're not giving me orders now, Frank! I come where I please and I go where I please! Remember that!"

He swept his hot eyes back to Janet for a fleeting second; then dug spurs into the black and went on toward the town at a run. Garland turned his head to watch—then swung back with his lips making a hard thin line against the brown of his face.

"Get along, McNair," he said curtly. "It's late."

As if to verify his statement, the dull boom of the evening gun drifted out from Fort Duncan a half mile away and Garland saw the flag coming down from the pole in front of headquarters while the faint notes of a trumpet came in on the wind. Corporal McNair grunted sourly, "Hup, Bess! Sam! Get along there!" and whipped the team into a trot again.

The cap'n will kill Arco Blaine one of these days, Corporal McNair was thinking behind the impassive redness of his face. *I hope to hell that McNair is around to see that.*

For Arco Blaine—Lieutenant Arco Blaine, then—had been drummed out of the service after the Fort Corse raid, Corporal McNair knew. The lieutenant had been drunk in his quarters when that had happened. If he'd been on the alert the skeleton garrison, left behind when the other companies had taken the field, wouldn't have been surprised. That was the way that Corporal McNair had heard it. And then, maybe, that stray bullet would not have killed the cap'n's pretty wife—it had been a sad thing for

21

Cap'n Frank Garland to find when K had finally come in from the fall campaign.

Janet and Frank Garland rode in silence for five minutes and then the girl broke into Frank's preoccupation to say slowly, "You were unfriendly. Who was that man?"

"Arco Blaine," Garland told her. "He is the kind that this country can do without, Miss Davenport."

Janet turned then and gave Garland a long, steady look. "You are rough with others, aren't you, Captain Garland?" she asked finally. "Was it that way with Gil?"

"Maybe," Garland said noncommittally. "I will leave the answer to that to Lieutenant Hardin." He let the matter end there.

Corporal McNair said suddenly, "There's K's scout comin' in, sorr."

Garland had already seen.

A slender column of riders was winding up out of the willows of Cache Creek and was turning into the main gate of Fort Duncan now. The distance was still great but not so great that Frank Garland couldn't see the fatigue which lay in the drooped, dusty shoulders of the troopers; in the stumbling gait of the troop horses as they plodded dispiritedly through the coming dusk. Two led horses were in the center of the column, the bodies of their riders roped—head and feet down, for that is the only way which a dead man may be packed—across the McClellan saddles.

Garland swore deep in his throat; steadied the girl beside him as McNair, not waiting for orders, whipped the team into a plunging run. The men were dismounting in front of K's stables as the wagon rolled up and Garland dropped into the dust.

"Take Miss Davenport to Major Kingman's quarters, McNair," he said shortly over his shoulder and then went on across the loose dirt, his face grim.

Sergeant Brecheen, a lanky man with the indelible marks of long service on him, saluted as he came up. Garland took in the scene with a swift glance. The jaded horses; the sagging troopers with the gauntness of hard

22

riding and harder fighting deep on them; the discolored bandage which was bound about Brecheen's upper arm where the shirt sleeve had been cut away. The two still figures had been taken from the saddles and now lay covered with two blankets, hunched and grotesque and sadly stiffened into the positions of their last ride.

"Who are they?" Garland asked.

"Troopers Benson an' Jarvis, sir," Sergeant Brecheen said quietly, bitterness in his voice.

Garland said curtly, "Tell Bestwood to have them taken to the hospital," but First Sergeant Jim Bestwood was already coming around the corner of the barracks, the last of the day lighting his craggy, solid face.

"I'll take care of it," he said.

Garland nodded and swung back to Brecheen. He noted, with a swift flaring of temper, that Corporal McNair had not gone on to Major Kingman's quarters as he had been ordered; instead, he had pulled the light wagon up some thirty yards away. Janet Davenport was getting down and coming toward the little knot of men who stood in front of the stables. She should not be here, Garland thought irritably, but he had more important things to attend to now.

"What happened, sergeant?" he demanded of Brecheen. "Where's Lieutenant Hardin?"

He saw the look which suddenly came into Brecheen's eyes and it warned him a little—deepened that feeling of foreboding which had ridden him all day. "The lieutenant didn't come back with us, sir," Brecheen answered slowly and Garland watched the anger crawl slowly up into the sergeant's wind-roughened face.

"What do you mean?" he demanded roughly. "He didn't come back with you! Where is he? Dead?"

He was vaguely aware that Janet was standing there hanging on Brecheen's answer, and he turned his head and said curtly, "Please go back to the wagon, Miss Davenport. This is not a woman's business."

"I have a right to know about Gil," she retorted.

Garland threw an angry glance at Corporal McNair, waiting flushed and uncomfortable in the wagon.

Well, let her stay, he decided dourly. If she wanted it the hard way, that was the way that she could have it. There were other women whose husbands and sweethearts hadn't come back from a scout into Indian country. Plenty of them.

He swung back to Brecheen. "Well?" he demanded.

Sergeant Brecheen ran a dirty hand across the stubble on his face. "The Sioux took him, sir," he said finally in a flat, emotionless voice.

"Prisoner?"

Brecheen nodded. "He was alive the last we seen of him."

Anger blossomed redly in Garland as the impact of that struck him. "Why didn't you get him back? K Company isn't in the habit of giving up prisoners to the Sioux! Wait for me in the orderly room, Brecheen!"

He swung away.

The sun was wholly gone now and the first faint wind of the evening was beginning to come up, bearing a reluctant promise of coolness on its breath. Janet Davenport was still standing there, her eyes shocked and unseeing as she stared beyond Garland.

"You sent him, captain," she said finally and there was something deeply accusing, wholly unforgiving in her voice now. "You sent him—when he was supposed to meet me."

"It is something that cannot be helped now," Frank Garland told her shortly. "He's probably all right, Miss Davenport." Then he added bitterly under his breath, "That is something that cannot be said for Troopers Benson and Jarvis."

He saw the faint shock that passed across her eyes; guessed that she hadn't realized the truth about them before. Well, they didn't teach you in New York or Baltimore or Boston—or wherever it was that she came from— that men sometimes got killed when they went into Indian country. Who, back there, could teach her?

"Those men in the wagon——" she asked hesitantly.

"Dead, Miss Davenport," Garland said bluntly. "I think that we had better go to Major Kingman's quarters now. Mrs. Kingman will be able to help you more than I can."

"You cannot help me at all, Captain Garland," she answered and her words were flat and bitter.

They went across the parade ground, Garland shortening his long stride to match the girl's and they did not speak again. He was glad that this was so. His mind was already dwelling darkly on the things that Sergeant Brecheen had told him. The news of Gil's capture—the fact that Gil was now in danger, possibly dead—left him strangely unmoved. It was Troopers Jarvis and Benson who occupied his thoughts as he swung along beside Janet Davenport. And, without his willing it so, the faces of the two men kept pushing up before him. Yet he had known them only as a good officer knows those who ride under his command.

The outward things about them; their quality as soldiers, the manner in which they cared for their arms and the zeal with which they tended their mounts. The proficiency that they had shown on the firing range and the number of times that they had gotten into trouble in the bars of Hagar. And, most important of all, the steadiness that had been theirs in battle. Those were the yardsticks against which a soldier was measured.

Benson, private—a dour man who had talked little and drank too much but who had halted to kick a foot loose from a stirrup and haul Corporal Lejune up behind him on that red day when Reno's command had fled through the valley of the Little Big Horn. Trooper Jarvis—recruit, walking out with Sergeant Helfron's pretty daughter down on Laundry Row. That was really all that he knew about them as individuals, as men, Frank Garland thought soberly.

There would be two letters to write tonight; letters to someone waiting back there behind the curtain which screened off the civilian world. For it was right that a man—every man—should have someone who cared a little and who waited to learn the fate that had finally over-taken him.

And then it came with a little shock to Frank Garland that there was now no one who really cared whether or not *he* lived or died. The thought gave him a queer, gray feeling of detachment as he glanced sideways at the girl who walked silently beside him. Gil Hardin was the lucky one, he thought sardonically. What Gil Hardin had done—whether he had behaved badly or well—did not matter now. In spite of it, someone cared.

They turned into Officers' Row; came presently to the end of it, to the house which Major Kingman occupied. Marjory Kingman, a faded but wholly serene woman, was coming down the steps, her hands outstretched to Janet.

"My dear," she was saying, "I am so glad that you have come. I'm Marjory Kingman—this is Caleb."

Frank Garland stood a little to one side, his hat in his hand while he waited, and Major Kingman came after a moment to draw him to the porch's far end. Promotion had passed the major by and the years had put too much flesh onto his stocky frame but his eyes were still clear and blue and unafraid.

He said, keeping his voice low so that it didn't reach his wife and Janet, "Lieutenant Hardin is back from his scout up the Blackbird, Frank? I saw the column——"

"Sergeant Brecheen brought the patrol back in, sir," Garland interrupted, his voice harsh. "Brecheen reported that Lieutenant Hardin was captured by a Sioux war party near Benner's Creek. Probably Broken Feather's band. I'm going back to the company to get the details now."

Major Kingman lifted a hand to stroke the gray goatee at his chin and the blue of his eyes took on a deeper shade. "I shall want all of the facts, Frank," he said quietly. "As soon as you can conveniently get them, please. It is not usual for people of this command to be made prisoner by the Sioux—or by anyone else. Were there other casualties?"

"Privates Benson and Jarvis killed," Garland told him in a tight, angry voice. "Brecheen brought their bodies in.

Brecheen, himself, was wounded in the arm. Not too bad. He'll be ready to ride with K after Hardin tomorrow——I assume that K does ride tomorrow, major?"

Major Kingman studied that for a long moment. "I don't know yet, Frank," he said finally and with a faint worry in his voice. "I will decide that when you bring your full report. I would like that tonight."

"In an hour, I think," Garland said.

Major Kingman nodded and sighed with his breath going out heavily. "We've got trouble ahead, Frank," he murmured. "A lot of trouble. I have seen it coming and this will bring it to a head. I will conduct services for the two men at ten tomorrow morning. Too bad. Too bad."

"Yes, sir." Garland saluted and turned away. Marjory Kingman and Janet had disappeared into the house. As she had gone, the girl had allowed her eyes to slide dispassionately across Frank Garland. She had said nothing.

That was the way that it was to be, he guessed. Well, it didn't matter.

4. Of the Man Called Arco Blaine

ARCO BLAINE LIFTED his big black into a run. The wagon, in which Janet Davenport had ridden with Frank Garland lay behind him on the dusty road which led to Fort Duncan. But the bruising scorn which he had seen in Frank Garland's eyes and the whip of contempt which had been in Garland's voice roweled him now with a bitter spur.

Memory of that Fort Corse affair still haunted him for he had lost his head there. But other men had made mistakes—worse mistakes—and they still wore the blue. People had been hurt—killed—and he was sorry for that. But the story that he had been lying drunk in his quarters was a lie dreamed up by a sergeant who had hated him. Yet the court-martial had believed the sergeant and had stripped Lieutenant Arco Blaine of his commission—dismissed him in disgrace.

Perhaps he had had a drink or two—the love of whiskey was a thing that ran strong in him. But he had been on his feet when the raid came in. That was the kind of injustice that ran in the Army these days——

So his thoughts ran on bitterly.

Hagar's lone street opened in front of him, unpleasantly familiar again after the months he had been away, and he hauled up in front of the Deerfoot saloon, looped the black's reins over the hitch rail, and went on through the swinging doors.

The place was nearly empty. A small poker game was going at a table in one corner; two range riders dawdled over their drinks at the near end of the bar. The bartender, a thick man with the pastiness of indoors laid on his face, came deliberately, wiping his hands on a rag as he came.

"Arco Blaine, ain't it?" he asked in a wheezy voice. "Ain't seen you in some time."

"Let that go," Arco told him roughly. "I didn't come here for conversation. Just set out the whiskey, Finn."

"Tryin' to be sociable," Finn mumbled in an aggrieved voice. "You got no need to tear a man's head off."

Arco Blaine turned the full weight of his stare on the other—resting his forearms on the bar's edge while his fingers tapped gently. "I said: *Bring me whiskey, Finn*," he repeated. Finn shook his head and slid out a bottle and a glass.

The two riders at the other end of the bar had dropped their casual talk and were staring curiously now, but Blaine paid no attention as he downed his drink and poured another. The whiskey bit warmly at his stomach; drove away, a little, the memory of Frank Garland's harshly accusing face.

They had been friends once.

Finn moved slowly back along the bar to where his other two customers waited. They were strangers to him— drifters with nothing to distinguish them except the brown of their faces and the marks of riding on them. Still, they were men to whom he could talk and right now Finn craved company.

"Feller seems to be on the prod, huh?" one of them asked. Finn mopped a little at the bar and glanced over his shoulder at Arco Blaine before replying.

"I don't monkey with 'em when they're like that," he said in his softly husky voice. "Not with fellers like Arco Blaine. He can be meaner than an August rattlesnake."

"Arco Blaine, huh?" one of the riders asked. "Ain't that the feller we heard about in Esperance, Pete?" He turned his attention back to Finn. "Does he run around some with a breed called Whitewater Charley—or would you know, friend?"

Finn's eyes suddenly became cautious above the fat of his cheeks. "I've heard that he does," he murmured. "That would mean something to you gents? Me, I don't

29

mix in Arco Blaine's business. It could be unhealthy—particular when he's drinking."

"Bad one, huh?" the rider called Pete asked. "I ain't much surprised, I guess. Not from what I heard in Esperance."

Finn thought that over for a moment and curiosity finally overcame his caution. "What'd you hear, friend?"

"Heard that he and this Whitewater Charley were peddlin' whiskey an' guns to the Sioux. Workin' on 'em to leave the reservation again. Make medicine for war, maybe. Me and Whitey, here, ain't fond of fellers like that. So I thought I'd ask."

"I don't know nothing," Finn said. "I stay healthy that way." He dropped his voice a notch lower. "I wasn't making no joke when I said he was a bad one. Two—three years ago he was court-martialed up to Fort Lincoln. Kicked out of the Army. Yep, pure bad in my book."

The poker game in the corner broke up in noisy argument and the players came to the bar, calling for drinks. Arco Blaine took his bottle and glass to a table where he could sit alone and look out of a dusty window and into Hagar's lone street. The two riders finished their tipple; went on out glancing curiously at Blaine as they passed.

He didn't notice as he sat with his shoulders hunched forward a little and both hands about his glass. The spark of anger became deeper at the back of his eyes as he thought back to what Major Kingman had said to him on his forbidden visit to Fort Duncan that afternoon.

Maybe he shouldn't have gone to Fort Duncan. Maybe he should not have showed his hand that way. But the desire to see old Kingman squirm had been too urgent in him. The trouble was that Major Kingman hadn't squirmed.

The old man was tough!

Lieutenant Oglethorpe Henderson had not been at his desk in the adjutant's office as Blaine had entered headquarters and that had been lucky because Thorpe would have made trouble sure. Blaine stalked across the small room; shouldered open the far door and went on into the room beyond. Major Kingman busy with a pile of papers, had waited to scrawl a signature before he had looked up. Then his eyes had gone hard as he recognized Arco Blaine and, in spite of himself, Arco had felt some of the brash confidence ooze out of him as he stopped to face the fierce old man across the littered desk.

Then Major Kingman demanded, spacing his words a little, "What are you doing here, Blaine? You should know better than to come to Fort Duncan again."

Arco Blaine had smiled tightly but inwardly he shrank from the ice in the major's eyes. Then he had remembered the document in the breast pocket of his coat and assurance had come back into him again. He made a cigarette for himself, set it alight, and allowed the smoke to escape between his lips in a thin trickle before he answered.

"I'm a civilian now," he said finally, putting insolence into his voice. "I go where I please. Remember, major?"

"I remember that I sat on the court-martial that drummed you out of the service," Major Kingman answered harshly, getting up to stand behind his desk. "It was on my recommendation that that court-martial decreed that you were never to set foot on a post of the United States Army again. I suggest that you leave now. I do not wish to have to call the guard."

His uneasiness in the major's presence had gone now, Blaine had thought triumphantly. Hell, he could handle the old man! He reached a hand into his pocket to reassure himself that that paper was still there.

"I wouldn't call the guard just yet, major," he said thinly, narrowing his eyes a little. "You and I have got a few things to talk about first."

"I have got nothing to talk about with you, Mr. Blaine," Major Kingman said coldly. "Get off Fort Duncan. Don't come back. That is my last word."

"I don't think so," Blaine said, suddenly angry. He reached into his pocket, pulled out the folded order which bore the seal of the War Department, and flipped it across the desk. "I think you had better read that, major, before

31

you start yelling for the guard. It might save you a lot of embarrassment."

For a moment, Major Kingman had stared at him across the desk, his eyes flinty and his mouth grim. Then, like a man doing a task wholly distasteful to him, he spread it open on the desk and looked down at it.

It was a communication, written in flowery language, directing that commanding officers of all posts and stations in the Dakota Territory would render all possible aid and assistance to the bearer, Mr. Arthur Blanding, in the furtherance of certain Indian affairs on which he was presently engaged. He would be treated as the personal representative of Senator Mark Hardin, of the Committee on Indian Affairs and would be permitted to accompany troops into the field in cases where he deemed that to be necessary in the furtherance of his mission. It was signed by an assistant Secretary of War.

Major Kingman, looking up with his eyes puzzled, did not doubt the authenticity of the signature. He had seen letters like this before. To his sorrow—for Washington, two thousand miles removed from the frontier, had little knowledge and less care for the problems which the Army faced out here. That was Washington's way.

"Who is this Mr. Arthur Blanding, sir?" he asked Blaine and thought, with a faint tightening of the muscles of his stomach, that he already knew the answer.

Blaine grinned sardonically. "I told you, when you cashiered me three years ago, that I had friends in Washington, major," he had said. "I told you also that I'd be back. Let us just say that Mr. Arthur Blanding is a good friend of mine. A very good friend of mine, I might say."

"I know no Arthur Blanding," Major Kingman said heavily. "As far as I am concerned, there is no Arthur Blanding, Mr. Blaine. Good day, sir."

Arco Blaine dragged deep on his cigarette; dropped the butt carelessly to the floor. "All right," he had said, enjoying this, "*I'm* Arthur Blanding. At least that is the name by which I am known to Senator Mark Hardin, major. Are

32

you going to honor that order or shall I report back to the senator that you refuse?"

"I shall not honor that order," Major Kingman said. "You can report what you please and to whom you please, Mr. Blaine. Meanwhile, you will leave Fort Duncan."

"You kicked me out of the Army," Blaine said between his teeth then. "Now I shall have the pleasure of doing the same to you, major. Mark Hardin is not a man to be trifled with. You will find that out."

Major Kingman's shoulders squared a little beneath the faded blue of his coat—squared as they had done at West Point nearly forty years gone now. "That may be, sir," he said calmly. "Until then, I am in command here. You are a fraud, a man whom I was once unfortunate enough to have had under my command. A man dismissed from the Army for drunkenness and cowardice. I do not wish to see you again, sir. You will leave this post and you will not come back. Have I made myself perfectly clear?"

Again that creeping uncertainty laid its cold fingers on Arco Blaine. For a moment longer he stood there, trying to stare the old man down. But his own eyes looked away first. Then he snatched up the order; stuffed it back into his pocket and whirled out of headquarters and into the sunlight of the parade ground where he had once ridden by, right at the head of his own company. Where he was now a scorned outcast.

The black had grunted, shied skittishly as Blaine had lurched blindly at him; then Blaine was in the saddle and spurring crazily away. The sentry on No. 1 Post called urgently to him as he went through the gate but Blaine had paid no attention and lifted the horse into a plunging run toward Hagar. A mile lay behind him before he had finally pulled the black down and jogged on at a trot toward the army wagon which was coming toward him.

These were the thoughts that Arco Blaine was thinking as he sat at the table in the Deerfoot saloon and looked out into the drabness of Hagar's street. A man tormented by devil's fishhooks which had snagged him and now held

33

him fast. Pride. Arrogance. Anger. And a sorrow, which he would not admit even to himself, for the position that he had lost, the courage that he had never had. The things that Frank Garland possessed—integrity, honor, the respect of other men—he still coveted with a fierceness which was intensified by the knowledge that they could never be his.

The afternoon died and the bartender lighted the swinging oil lamps. More men were coming into the Deerfoot now, boisterous with full bellies and the thought of the evening's play ahead of them but Blaine paid no attention.

The bottle was empty and he signalled for Finn to bring another. He was not drunk. Whiskey had long since lost its power to thicken his tongue or unsettle his gait. It did something worse. It started those little worms to crawling in his brain again. So he sat in his corner now, smiling a little and lifting his glass with deliberate fingers, a man peering into the smoky depths of an abyss which opened its bottomless maw before him. There were faces down there in the swirling mists which peered accusingly up at him. Faces twisted with pain. Sergeant major Hewlett was there, dead from a half-dozen knife wounds as he had tried to drag himself out of the hospital to lead the rally which Lieutenant Arco Blaine should have led. Private Jed Smith, scalped and with a Sioux arrow through him. Martha Garland——

For he had killed them at Fort Corse and now he was an outcast, damned to walk alone until the smoke of that abyss reached up to close wraithlike arms around him and pull him down. . . .

Blaine swore and reached again for the bottle. He was vaguely aware that Finn was standing over him, the man's beefy face a little wary. "Well?" he asked sharply.

"Whitewater Charley wants to see you," Finn said. "Sent word it's important. He's at the hotel," and turned away abruptly as though glad that his errand was over.

For a moment Blaine studied that; then grunted softly and pushed himself away from the table and stood. He went steadily toward the swinging doors, men making a lane for him as he walked, and the night air felt good against his face as he emerged into the starlight and turned down the street.

The hotel clerk, a cadaverous man with drooping mustaches, looked at Arco as he entered. "Whitewater's up in your room," he spoke curtly and turned away.

There was a creaky stair, which bent—right-angled—half-way up, and then a dim and musty corridor and a door with the number 202 painted crudely on it—and Blaine went in. Whitewater Charley lay on the single bed, boots on and spurs tangled in the sleazy blanket. Now he sat up awkwardly, a squat man with a swarthy, pock-marked face.

"Got news," he grunted. "Figured you'd want to hear it an' the Deerfoot wasn't no place to tell you."

Blaine hooked a chair around with the toe of his boot, sat in it and stared indifferently across the rickety table. "What news?" he asked thinly.

Whitewater Charley twisted his head around and spat through the open window. "I been talkin' to one of the soldiers from the post," he said. "Young Gil Hardin didn't come back from that scout today. This feller said that Broken Feather had captured the lieutenant up on Benner's Creek day before yesterday."

Arco Blaine suddenly sat straight in his chair, the cobwebs of the whiskey washed away leaving his brain sharp and clear. "You sure of that?" he asked sharply.

"It's what the soldier said," Whitewater Charley grunted. "Why would he lie—the Army ain't happy about it."

Blaine suddenly smiled tightly, placed his hands flat on the table. "So Broken Feather's scooped up the senator's son," he said softly, speaking half to himself. "Now, that puts a sort of a different face on things, doesn't it?"

"Broken Feather will probably fry him," Whitewater Charley said without concern. "The chief ain't got any love for the pony soldiers and he figures that his medicine's plenty powerful now that he has got away from the reservation."

Arco Blaine's face hardened suddenly. "I want young Hardin kept alive," he said harshly. "For the time being, anyway. You know where Broken Feather's holed up, Charley?"

"Place that the Injuns call 'Hole-that-Hides', I think," Whitewater Charley said. "Three day ride back into the hills an' a hell of a place to get to."

Blaine slapped a palm down hard on the table and jerked himself out of his chair. He crossed the room and stood looking down into the street. A street that he hated, he thought, moistening his lips a little with his tongue. A street to which he had come because of one careless mistake three years ago.

Well, maybe this was the break that he had been waiting for! With Gil Hardin in his hands he could demand that the Army give him the vindication that he wanted, his commission back, the right to walk proudly again. For Gil Hardin was the apple of Senator Mark Hardin's eye—and Senator Mark Hardin was a power in Washington.

Yes, this might be the break!

Then his face darkened suddenly again for he knew that Frank Garland would never permit those things to come to pass. Well, he'd look to Frank Garland in due course.

He turned sharply to Whitewater Charley. "Get word to Feather that I want him to hang on tight to young Hardin. Keep him unharmed. Tell Feather that the lieutenant is worth a hundred ponies to his father. I will promise that. Got it, Charley?"

Whitewater Charley grunted his assent. "Want me to go myself, Arco?"

Blaine thought that over for a long moment, scowling at the smoking lamp in its bracket against the wall.

"You got anybody else you can trust?"

"Jim White Eagle. He's a cousin of mine. Pretty good man in the hills."

"Send him then," Blaine said decisively. "Frank Garland will be in town tonight. I may want you around."

Whitewater Charley spat again. "I'd rather ride after

Broken Feather," he said sourly. "Frank Garland's bad medicine, in my book."

"He's beef the same as anybody else once you're behind him with a gun," Blaine said cryptically. "Anyway, you stick around. Tomorrow I may want you to take a letter out to a lady at Fort Duncan for me."

"Why don't you take it yourself?"

Arco Blaine grinned tightly. "I'm not exactly welcome at Duncan right now," he said softly. "Give me a little time though, Charley, and I'll own that place."

5. "We Charged. That's All I Know"

NIGHT WAS already beginning to spread over the parade ground as Frank Garland left Major Kingman standing on the low porch of the commanding officer's quarters. For a moment the major watched as Frank moved on across to where the barracks lay; then the old man sighed a little and went on back into the house.

Here, Marjory Kingman had made a home with a woman's infinite care; a haven of familiar and reassuring landmarks, to which a man could turn after the buffetings of this raw land. The settee had come from the Philadelphia house and the carved sideboard and the silver candlesticks had been a wedding present. The china lamp, roses making a splash of color on its shade, stood on the claw-footed table in the room's center. Curtains, once gay but faded now by the remorseless sunlight of this country, softened the windows and by the fireplace was Caleb's easy chair. For Marjory Kingman was an Army wife—one of the unsung who followed their men, making a life for them wherever they might go.

She came now, closing the door which led to Janet Davenport's room gently behind her and moved across the room to place her hand on her husband's arm as he stood looking down at the fireplace. "It's bad, isn't it, Caleb? I heard what Frank told you."

"It's bad, Maggie," the major said. He lowered himself into the chair and thoughtfully began to stuff tobacco into his pipe. "It's always bad when any of our people are taken by the Sioux. The fact that it was young Hardin makes it worse."

"Because of his father—the senator?"

Major Kingman nodded, waiting to reply until he had gotten his pipe lighted and drawing. "The senator is on his way here for Gil's wedding and he won't be pleased at the news we have for him. I cannot blame him for that. It is the form that his displeasure will likely take that is bothering me now."

"He will relieve you from command of Fort Duncan?" Marjory Kingman asked quietly.

Her husband jerked an impatient hand. "Probably. That is not important. What is important is that I have good reason to suspect that, for his own ends, Mark Hardin wishes the Army to take the field against the Indians again. That would be tragedy now. I must prevent it if I can."

"And can you, Caleb?"

"Mark Hardin is a hard, vindictive man and Gil's capture will give him the excuse which he has been looking for, I'm afraid. I'll know better what to do after I've had Frank's report later tonight. Talked with Frank. How is Janet taking it, Maggie?"

"I don't know," Marjory Kingman said thoughtfully. "I honestly don't know, Caleb. She is shocked—and terribly bitter at Frank Garland, I think. Perhaps you will talk to her later?"

Major Kingman nodded, smoke from his pipe curling up past the heavy lines of his face. "Yes, I'll do that. There is nothing else that Frank could have done in this matter, Maggie."

"We both know that," Marjory Kingman answered. "But Janet Davenport does not. Perhaps she never will."

He was fond of Major Kingman, Frank Garland was thinking as he neared the barracks. Liked him—and pitied him a little. For the major was a man who had worn the blue all of his adult life; a man who had served his country faithfully and well and who deserved better of it than to spend the last years of his service here on an obscure frontier outpost. Not that the major would have it different, Frank admitted—that was the mark of the man—but there was small reward in being forgotten here, faced with an

39

impossible task and handcuffed by the intrigue of Washington.

Politicians, like Gil Hardin's father, fostered that intrigue for their own ends. And presently the telegraph wire would be burning with frantic messages. Orders concerning the capture of Lieutenant Gilbert Hardin—scion of Mark Hardin, the shaggy bear—who had led a scout up the Blackbird and who had gotten two men killed and himself made prisoner by the Sioux.

Garland's lips set angrily. There would be no telegraph wires burning over Troopers Benson and Jarvis, he thought. They would go into the ground with a few meaningless words mumbled over them—two letters written and then no one would remember. Except maybe the flaxenhaired little girl down on Suds Row; or some shadowy and unknown person out there beyond the frontier's curtain who once might have cared for Trooper Benson.

For Benson and Jarvis were not important in Washington. They were just soldiers. Men who drew their few dollars at the pay table each month; men what ate their beans and hardtack and were supposed to be grateful for that. Troopers—just troopers. And troopers were expendable in this hard land.

Garland swore and shook the thought away.

He came now to the barracks, noisy with men who had been fed and who lay on their bunks and dreamed or who splashed in from the washroom or played poker in the corner, arguing noisily over women and fights that were gone and over furloughs yet to come. For that was the way with soldiers, Frank Garland thought, and it was good.

He paused for a moment at the path to the orderly room and a quick surge of pride ran through him. This was his company. Company K. Sixty-five men, each with his own ambitions and dreams. There were the bad and the good among that sixty-five. The embezzler, who had fled his peculations just ahead of the law in some unknown city, and the country boy who had left the monotony of the farm for the adventure which the uniform promised him. The shy kid who wrote long letters to a girl back home;

40

the hard-bitten soldier who had known the sound of the guns at Second Manassas and who brawled through Hagar on payday.

But, when the clear notes of the trumpet rippled out in the chill morning; when they slipped carbines into boots, stood to horse, and swung up into saddles; when the racketing notes of the *charge* tore out of the brassy throats of the horns—then they were "K", as good a company as a man could want. Better, maybe. It was those things—and other things like them—that kept a man staying on out here, eating the alkali dust of the summers and freezing in the chill of the winters, Garland thought.

First Sergeant Jim Bestwood, shadowy in the first of the starlight, came around the corner of the barracks and moved slowly toward him, saluting with the ease of long practice as he came. A good man, Bestwood.

"Evening, Captain," he said.

Garland returned the salute; nodded, his mind wrenched abruptly back to the things before him. "Is Brecheen in the orderly room, Jim?" he asked.

"I sent him off to get chow," Bestwood answered. "He's pretty well beat. Ought to be back by now, though."

"How's his arm?"

"It'll do—he'll be able to ride tomorrow," Bestwood said. Then he added—the same thing that Garland had said to Major Kingman earlier—"I take it K does ride tomorrow?"

"The major hasn't said," Frank Garland told him shortly. "I'll get orders later tonight."

He wondered a little if he had really detected a faintly accusing note in Bestwood's voice; wondered if Jim, too, thought that he had made a mistake in entrusting two squads of K to Gil Hardin. Gil had not been liked in the company—a martinet who made no attempt to hide the low esteem in which he held enlisted ranks. Well, he had made a mistake, Garland guessed sourly, but it was too late to start crying about that now.

"A nasty business," Jim Bestwood was saying. "Ain't much that we can do except go out an' try to get the lieu-

41

tenant back, I guess. If Broken Feather's braves leave anything for us to get."

Frank Garland said abruptly, "That's right," and swung away toward the door to the orderly room. Off to his left the low rumble of barracks noise lifted and fell as men settled down to the evening.

Men were drifting back into the long barrack room as Private Paul Fraley sat down on his bunk and put his elbows on his knees and stared at the hard-packed earth of the floor in front of him. He had washed away the red dirt of the last five days; dragged a comb through the tight mop of his curly hair but the shock of what had happened day before yesterday still held him.

It had been Private Fraley's first fight—a rough affair while it had lasted. Naked and yelling men who had boiled up out of nowhere; the racket of gunfire and the cries of men going down. And now he had the memory of Georgie Jarvis roped across his saddle, lying twisted beneath a blanket an hour ago. Later those pictures would fade a little but they were too vivid right now.

Corporal Tim O'Garragh, red-faced and hard-bitten and ten years older than Fraley's nineteen, sat down on the bunk opposite and watched the boy with an expressionless stare. A poker game started noisily farther along the big room and Monk Walters, K's trumpeter, called, "Hey, Dutch! You want to go into town with me tonight?" Sergeant Brecheen, face impassive and a fresh bandage on his arm, passed by on his way to the orderly room.

"What happened, kid?" Corporal O'Garragh asked softly then. "What about Benson and Jarvis?"

Fraley shook his head dumbly, the yellow light sliding across the scrubbed planes of his face. "I don't know," he said in a voice which was little more than a whisper. "We come up a little draw and out onto a ridge and there was a bunch of lodges. I don't know how many. Maybe fifty. They were down in the valley below us. Everything happened awful fast after that."

"Yeah," Corporal O'Garragh said drily. "It usually

42

does. Fifty lodges could mean maybe twice that many braves. A hell of a lot to handle with two squads of cavalry. They jumped you, huh?"

"We jumped them," Private Fraley said, keeping his eyes on the dirt floor. "Lieutenant Hardin swings his arm up and yells *Charge!* and we ride right into the middle of 'em."

For a moment a faint shock showed in Tim O'Garragh's flat, gray eyes and there was disbelief in his voice as he asked again, "You charged 'em! Just like that?"

"Just like that," Fraley answered.

"You didn't scout 'em first? You didn't——"

"We didn't do nothing that I know of," Fraley said tiredly. "We just charged. There was another bunch waitin' for us up in a little side canyon. They got us when we were going in. That's all I know about it, corporal."

Corporal O'Garragh whistled tunelessly between his teeth for a moment, paying no attention to a man who was calling his name from the far end of the room. Then he said with a swift and bitter violence, "So young Lieutenant Hardin was lookin' for glory again, was he? I am not surprised. I guess it was that he wished to shine mightily in the eyes of his woman when she arrived this afternoon— and now Benson and Jarvis are lying out in the ice house waitin' for their burying tomorrow! Damn the man's eyes! I hope that the Sioux cut his hair!"

Private Fraley said nothing more as the corporal got to his feet, glanced angrily down the length of the long room, and started to move away. After two steps, O'Garragh paused; came back to drop a hand on the boy's shoulder.

"You and Jarvis were pals, kid?"

"We came from the same town," Fraley told him in a muffled voice. "We went to Jefferson Barracks together to enlist. I—liked him, I guess."

O'Garragh nodded. "It is a hard thing," he said and some of the flinty carelessness had gone out of his voice. "It is a thing, though, that you will get over. That must be the way of it, man, for it's all a part of what you bought

43

when you held up your hand in Jefferson Barracks and said the words. Can you see that, boy?"

"I guess so," Fraley answered, his voice scarcely audible. "I guess I got to see it."

Corporal O'Garragh nodded and was gone, then, and Fraley heard him tossing rough banter with the men who sat about the poker table. For a moment longer, Fraley sat on his bunk, his elbows on his knees. Then he got up slowly and went on out into the night which had closed down over Fort Duncan.

Lights were winking on in the windows of the officers' quarters across the parade ground and the wind had chilled with the coming of the night; in it, stronger now, was that hint of winter which lay just around the corner. Young Fraley had never seen winter in this country and he was a little afraid of it. He shivered a little as he paused in the shadows and lonesomeness came to settle its full impact on him with an icy grip.

Then a cigar end glowed in the shadows and First Sergeant Jim Bestwood came across the packed ground from the orderly room where Garland was conferring with Sergeant Brecheen and Toronto Peters, the civilian scout who had accompanied K's two squads up the Blackbird. Bestwood saw Fraley, gave him a sharp regard for a moment, and stepped up beside him.

"Where would you be going tonight, son?" he asked in a not unkindly voice. "I would expect that after five days hard riding you'd be hitting your bed sack tonight—not heading for the town."

Young Paul Fraley fidgeted a little nervously. He was vaguely afraid of First Sergeant Bestwood—a grim, saturnine soldier who had been taking the Army's pay before Fraley had been born. A severe, testy man; swift in his judgments and inexorable in their executions. Now, though, Sergeant Jim Bestwood was something tangible to tie to and young Paul Fraley needed that.

"I wasn't going to town, sergeant," he said. "I was just going to—walk around, I guess."

44

"Down to Suds Row, maybe?" Sergeant Bestwood hazarded in a dry voice. "I would be right?"

"Yes, sir. You're right, I guess."

"You have got a girl down there, Fraley?"

Paul Fraley shook his head miserably; shuffled his feet a little against the hard earth. "No, sir. I haven't got a girl. I never had one, I guess. Jarvis, he wanted me to go. After he got hit, he gave me a trinket—a necklace, sort of, that he wanted me to give to a girl down there——"

The end of Jim Bestwood's cigar glowed redly in the semidarkness and some of the rough edge had gone from his voice when he spoke again. "A hard task that Private Jarvis gave you, son," he said finally. "A hard task. Still, it has to be done. You'd best go now and get it over with." He wheeled and went on back in the direction of the orderly room.

The stars seemed to be dropping lower in the sky as Private Fraley turned into Suds Row—the line of noncommissioned officers' quarters which stretched south from the commissary building. Fraley moved slowly, dreading the moment when he must come to the house where Annie Helfron lived. It was midway along the row and he paused for a moment in front of it, mustering his courage; then went slowly up to knock. Annie Helfron came to the door, apple-cheeked and with the light behind her making a halo about her corn-colored hair. He could see from her eyes that she already knew about Georgie Jarvis and then she came on out into the starlight, drawing the door closed behind her as she came.

"I hoped that it would be you, Paul," she said so softly that he scarcely heard her. Now that he was here he could think of nothing to say; felt tongue-tied and miserable and wished that he had stayed back in the barracks. He had fallen in love with Annie Helfron on that first day when Georgie had introduced them a month ago—and now he had come to tell her about Georgie, whom Annie had loved instead. Then Annie was asking quietly, "You came about Georgie, didn't you, Paul?" and the soft sound of her voice seemed to make everything all right again, Paul Fraley thought.

She took his arm with a matureness beyond her seventeen years and led him on out into the cool evening. They turned into the baked path which led toward the main guard gate, walking slowly now, not saying anything for a moment.

Fraley spoke finally. "George wanted you to have this, Annie," he said and drew the trinket—a tiny medal on a chain—from his pocket and put it into her hand. She stood there looking at it for a long moment in the starlight and Paul was suddenly acutely aware of the elusive fragrance of her hair and of the glow which the faint light made on the roundness of her face.

"You were fond of George, weren't you, Paul?" she asked and again her voice was so low that Fraley could barely hear it.

He said, "Yes, I—liked him, Annie."

"I know how it is," she murmured. "I loved George, Paul. But not in the way that he wanted it. More like a brother. He seemed so lost. So lonesome."

"I guess that everybody is lonesome," Fraley said, his words running together a little.

"Are you lonesome, Paul?"

"I guess so. Now that Georgie——" Suddenly she was in his arms, her face pressed close against his own and her lips smothering the words.

"Don't be lonesome, Paul," she whispered fiercely. "I can't stand it if you are. Don't ever be lonesome again!"

He held her so for a long moment; tenderly—for he had never held a girl in his arms before. And he was thinking, his mind whirling crazily: *Why, I came here to try and help Annie but she is the one who is helping me, instead.*

Then she lifted her head slowly and said, "Come back soon, Paul. Don't ever stay away. Please!" and kissed him gently on the mouth and then was gone, running in the night toward where the lights of Suds Row made a cheerful pattern against the darkness. Warm, friendly lights now, Paul Fraley thought.

Corporal Tim O'Garragh, furrows wrinkling his fore-head, moved on out of the barracks and walked slowly to where the stables made a squat bulk in the evening. The warm, acrid odor inside cheered him a little as he moved among the horses until he came to his own mount. He slapped the horse affectionately on the rump; the animal snorted, butted a head at O'Garragh's shoulder and the corporal swore without rancor and moved away.

A lantern made a swinging, shifting light at the far end of the long low building and O'Garragh went toward it. Then Corporal McNair's gravelly voice called harshly, "Who's there?" and Tim O'Garragh answered, "O'Garragh, Mac. And don't give me the rough of your tongue like that, man."

He moved on until he stood in the little circle of radiance which fell about Corporal McNair, who was acting stable sergeant. McNair grunted and put the lantern down while he worried a chew of tobacco from a plug and passed the plug across to O'Garragh.

"Gettin' spooky, I guess," he admitted. "A bad business up there on the Blackbird, Tim."

"Bad enough," O'Garragh said. "Nothing that surprised me too much, though. Not with the young Mister Hardin in command."

McNair thought that over but made no comment. He said, then, abruptly changing the subject, "Arco Blaine's back. We run into him when I was driving Cap'n Garland an' the lieutenant's young lady back from town this after-noon. The cap'n and Arco had words."

"Ah," O'Garragh murmured softly. "They did that, did they?"

"Cap'n Garland warned the man to be out of town this night," McNair grunted. "Gave him the whip, O'Garragh. The cap'n promised that he would be in town to see that he was gone."

It was Corporal O'Garragh's turn to fall silent for a long moment now. Then he said finally, "It is not good for Frank Garland to go alone. Maybe it would be just as well if O'Garragh rode into Hagar tonight, too."

47

"I had some such thought," McNair said.

"I have spoken nothing to you, McNair," O'Garragh murmured softly. "And you will be blind and dumb should you see a horse leave the stables later on this night."

"A bat could not be blinder," Corporal McNair said, spitting. "Luck ride with you, Timmy."

6. It Happened on the Blackbird

TORONTO PETERS, a lanky and hard-bitten man—old with
riding and wise in the ways of Indian fighting—sat in the
first sergeant's cubbyhole of an office as Garland and Jim
Bestwood came into the orderly room. Garland said, "Evening, Pete. Come on in as soon as Brecheen gets here.
I'll want you, too, Jim," and passed on into his own office
beyond.

Bestwood dropped his hat onto the rough table which
served him as a desk and moved his attention back to
Toronto Peters. "Brecheen ain't back from chow yet?" he
asked.

"Ought to be comin' now," Toronto grunted. "Looks
like we got some pieces to pick up, Jim."

Bestwood gave him a glance which was faintly irritated.
"I been picking up pieces for close to forty years now," he
said. "A man can get tired of it, Pete."

Toronto Peters leaned back, tipping his chair against the
wall on two legs while he grinned beneath his scraggly
mustache. A little wind came through the drafty door to
make the lamp flicker and smoke in its bracket against the
far wall; from beyond the door came the noises of the
barracks.

"Be nice if I had a dollar—even a Mex dollar—for every
time I've heard that song from you, Jim," Toronto said
laconically. "If I did, I'd retire an' buy me a saloon in St.
Louis an' live like a gentleman. Why in hell don't you get
out of the Army—it ain't no place for an old coot like you,
anyhow."

Jim Bestwood scowled for a moment, the heavy lines
deepening about his mouth; then shrugged his shoulders
and let his face relax. "Tried it once," he said. "Back in

49

sixty-six after the war. I went to farming for a year and damn near went crazy. When I saw a recruiting sergeant again I was just about ready to lick his boots. The Bestwoods wasn't born with much sense, I guess."

"Don't take it hard," Toronto said. "The Army'll give you a fine funeral when the Injuns finally lift your hair. I hear that Arco Blaine is back in Hagar, Jim."

The good humor went out of the first sergeant's face again, leaving it angry and a little disturbed. "I had heard so," he answered. "I don't like that, Pete. It will come to a shooting between him and Frank Garland one of these days."

Toronto Peters narrowed his eyes a little; tipped his chair down again while he fumbled in the pocket of his buckskin coat for his tobacco plug. There was a faint satisfaction on his face as he considered Bestwood's words.

"Frank will kill him," he said.

Sergeant Brecheen came in then, some of the tiredness washed out of his face by the hot meal that he had just finished. He stopped to look inquiringly at Bestwood and the first sergeant said roughly, "Come on. Let's get this done with."

Garland's office was a room little larger than the one that they had left. There was another table and a filing cabinet made out of an ammunition box and the single chair in which Frank Garland was sitting. K's guidon was in its stand against the wall beside a window which looked out over the dark parade ground. Sergeant Brecheen and Jim Bestwood ranged themselves beside the table; Toronto Peters squatted on his heels against the door, indifferent to anything that smelled of army discipline or army formality. Frank Garland didn't care.

"Start at the beginning," he said to Brecheen.

"There wasn't nothing unusual on the first day out," Brecheen said, his face twisted into a frown of concentration. "We camped on Golyer's Fork that night. The lieutenant didn't have much of anything to say but he acted queer. Like he had something on his mind, sir. Kind of hard to get along with. That right, Pete?"

50

"Like an old cow that'd lost her calf," Toronto Peters agreed sourly. "On the prod."

Garland nodded his head impatiently. "Get on with it—and never mind Lieutenant Hardin's disposition. I want to know what happened, Brecheen."

"I'm coming to it, sir," Sergeant Brecheen said. He was a phlegmatic man who couldn't be hurried. "We cut Indian sign well up the Blackbird maybe three o'clock the next afternoon. Not a war party, I figured. Pete figured the same."

"Feather's band," Toronto Peters grunted. "They'd left enough sign behind 'em to spell that out. An' Brecheen's right—it wasn't no war party. Marks of travois poles—a lot of lodges. Meant that Feather had his women and kids along with him."

"You told that to Lieutenant Hardin?" Garland asked, his voice sharp.

Brecheen nodded. "I told him," he said. "He said I was crazy. Then Pete told him."

"Told him again when we camped that night," Toronto Peters interposed sourly. "I never trusted that man—or liked him, neither." He stopped and scrubbed a hand across the bristles on his chin and then grinned. "I ain't hobbled by no regulations when it comes to talkin' back to wet-nosed lieutenants, Frank."

For a fleeting moment, Garland's grim expression eased a little; a faint mirth washed across his mouth. "I have observed that, Pete," he said. "One of these days some wet-nosed lieutenant will bend his saber over your head. Go on, Brecheen. What did Lieutenant Hardin decide about this Indian band?"

"Said we'd follow it for the rest of the afternoon. He'd decide what to do about it in the morning, sir," Sergeant Brecheen answered, disapproval of Gil Hardin's actions heavy in his voice. "So we camped that night back from the river, putting out a strong guard. I saw to that. The lieutenant was jumpy—pretty hard to get along with."

"Scared, in my book," Toronto Peters put in under his breath.

51

Frank Garland stopped him with an impatient hand. "Let it go, Pete. Brecheen, get to the fight."

"We marched again before daylight the next morning—that was day before yesterday, sir," Sergeant Brecheen said imperturbably. "I tried to find out what the lieutenant meant to do—for we was still following Broken Feather's trail—but the lieutenant didn't have no answers. Then Pete said maybe he'd better go on ahead and have a look-see and the lieutenant said never to mind that. We'd go on for another hour, he said. Then, if we hadn't caught up to the Indians yet, we'd turn and start back for Duncan.

"Just after daybreak we came to the top of a little ridge where Benner's Creek comes down to the Blackbird. There is a little valley just beyond and the Indians were camped there—maybe sixty lodges."

Sergeant Brecheen hesitated for a long moment—as though he was trying to make sure in his mind as to the way the thing had finally happened. Then he shook his head slowly; rubbed his chin with his fingers as he looked across the table.

"It is a thing that I cannot understand, sir," he answered. "The two squads was right behind us, bunched a little and I was waving them back into cover when the lieutenant——"

He went on, clipping his words a little now. The lieutenant had suddenly flung K's two squads into a skirmish line, drawn his saber and led a charge down onto the unsuspecting village below.

"We went through 'em," Brecheen said soberly. "There wasn't nothin' but squaws and kids there when we hit. Then maybe a hundred braves come hellin' out at us from a side canyon and we took it bad. Both Benson an' Jarvis were hit but they managed to hold their saddles until we got back across Benner's Creek. Feather didn't follow us. I don't know why."

"What about Hardin?" Garland asked tightly.

"He was out in front when the Injuns come out of the canyon. Headed straight for 'em an' it looked to me like his horse had run away," Toronto Peters grunted sourly. "The

Injuns gobbled him up. He wasn't dead the last I seen of him. He probably is by now."

"Why didn't you go back after him?" Sergeant Brecheen gazed stolidly at the officer across the table.

"I considered it, sir," he said. "I decided against it. There were close to a hundred braves in that party—we were outnumbered close to ten to one. If I'd tried to go back for the lieutenant, I'd have left every man of the two squads back there on Benner's Creek."

Frank Garland considered that soberly for a moment; then nodded slowly. He knew that Sergeant Brecheen was right—that he probably would have made the same decision under the circumstances. Memory still ran bright in the army of a commander who had rashly disregarded the realities of war and who had left the most of a good regiment lying—stripped and scalped and dead—on another creek which the Indians called the Greasy Grass but which was marked down on the Army's maps as the Little Big Horn.

"All right," he said finally, dismissing the subject. "I've got the picture, I guess, unless either of you have got anything more to add to it. Pete?"

Toronto Peters got slowly to his feet, stretched his stubby frame in the lamp's smoky light. "It ain't quiet all, Frank," he said laconically. "I never got around to tellin' Brecheen this. While he was takin' care of Benson and Jarvis and settin' up his defense in case Feather pushed the fight, I went back across Benner's Creek to snoop around a little. I'd seen a buck knocked off his horse as we come down from the ridge. He'd rolled into a little gully."

Toronto Peters paused for a moment, grinning wolfishly. "He was still there—had a bullet through his belly—so I asked him some questions. Mighty talkative for an Injun, Frank."

"I'm listening," Garland said tightly.

"Bad trouble comin'," Toronto said. "The Injuns have been told that the Army's going to put on a winter campaign this year—same as Custer pulled, down on the

Washita. The word is that all of the bands are to be rounded up when the snow gets deep and they can't take to the hills. Then the government is goin' to ship 'em all to some new reservation where they'll never see their old hunting grounds again. That's what this feller told me, Frank."

"That's the reason that Broken Feather left the reservation?"

"That's the reason. An' Feather is just the first. The rest are just waiting to see what happens. If Feather makes his play stick, the other bands will go out, too. The Uncpapas have already got war parties out in the hills."

"He tell you who has been spreading this rumor, Pete?"

"Yep," Toronto grunted. "Arco Blaine an' that breed that runs with Arco. But Arco ain't the kingpin in this business, Frank. It's somebody with more money and more pull than a cashiered lieutenant has got. Arco has been givin' the Injuns whiskey and guns—it takes money to do that."

Sergeant Bestwood added roughly, "The word is that Arco Blaine is back in Hagar, captain. I thought you should know."

Garland nodded. "I met him on the road coming out from town this afternoon," he said. He started to say something further; checked himself and then added, "See that K is ready to march tomorrow, if we get the word, Jim. Any of you have anything more?"

Jim Bestwood glanced at the other two; then shook his head. Garland got up from his chair, reaching for his hat. "Then good night," he said and went out the door.

The wind, coming out of the north now, was cold against his face as Garland went across the empty parade ground. There was a storm in the air, he thought absently; the unseasonable heat of the last few days presaged that. His mind returned, then, to the things that Brecheen and Toronto Peters had told him. What, he wondered, could have moved Gil Hardin to do the things that he had done up there on the Blackbird!

Had anger over his interview with Garland still been riding him? It was possible. Or had he simply lost his head in the stress of the moment? Garland didn't know—couldn't guess and he shrugged the thought impatiently away as he stepped onto the porch in front of Major Kingman's quarters.

Major Kingman greeted him at the door and led the way through the pleasant room, where a fire had now been kindled against the evening's chill, and on into the small room beyond which served as a study.

Garland sat in the chair beside the major's desk and dropped his hat onto the floor beside him. "I've got the story of what happened up on the Blackbird, sir," he said tiredly. "It's not pretty and it's not wholly understandable, either."

Major Kingman nodded and stuffed tobacco into his pipe and listened. When Garland had finished relating Gil Hardin's inexplicable behavior, he sighed gently. "Stubbornness, false pride, immaturity can lead a man to do such things, Frank," he said. "It was one of those, I suppose."

Garland leaned forward to put a big fist roughly onto the desk. "I've got an uglier word for it, major," he said bleakly. "Hardin's blunder cost the lives of two good men."

Major Kingman nodded soberly. "I wish that the thing could be undone," he said with an ineffable sadness running through his voice. "It can't. You've been out here for a long time, Frank. Do you read anything into this whole affair other than the Indians' discontent with the reservation—which placed Broken Feather's band up there on the Blackbird—and a young officer's failure of judgment when he discovered them?"

Garland then told of what Toronto Peters had learned about Arco Blaine. When he had finished, Major Kingman's face had settled into grim lines as he tamped a thumb at the bowl of his pipe.

"It all ties in, Frank," he said finally. "Arco Blaine was at Fort Duncan this afternoon. He forced his way into my office and I ordered him off the post."

He went on to tell of the order from the Department, and Frank Garland listened, his long legs thrust out in front of him and his dark face impassive. Anger glowed sharply in his eyes when the major mentioned the part of the order which had specified that the spurious Arthur Blanding would be allowed to ride with any columns which might take the field.

"He wouldn't ride a mile alive with K," he said curtly. "And Arco knows it. This thing is tangled into a messy knot, major. Do you make sense of it?"

Major Kingman nodded soberly; reached for his tobacco pouch. "I think I do. I have my own sources of information in Washington, Frank," he said. "They tell me that Mark Hardin is backing a syndicate which wants to get hold of new lands along the Yellowstone. They are barred now from the grab because those are treaty lands still. But, if the Sioux go to war again, it is likely that those lands will be declared forfeit—and the syndicate can move in."

Major Kingman stopped. Garland sat with his chin dropped to his chest while he studied the shadow which the major's desk cast on the floor. In the room beyond, a log crackled sharply in the fireplace. And somewhere a door opened softly and then closed again.

"Yes," Frank Garland said finally. "It adds up. Senator Hardin, from what I've heard of the man, has the power and the ruthlessness to do that. And he has sent Arco Blaine here with a phony alias—for the Department would never issue such papers to a man with Arco's record—to stir the tribes up. I had heard rumors but I thought that it was a whiskey or gunrunning scheme of Blaine's. I can see now that it was a lot more."

Major Kingman nodded a sober agreement. "There's a chance—a small one—that we may be able to head this thing off. If we should hit Broken Feather hard, scatter his band and bring him in as a prisoner to Duncan, we might break the backbone of this thing. It is likely that other bands would not care to make the attempt then."

"K is ready to march tomorrow morning," Frank Garland said tightly. "Or tonight, if you like. Time is important —Gil may already be dead."

"Lieutenant Hardin is not my concern right now," Major Kingman said, his voice hard. "My concern is to prevent a new and unjust war from starting out here again, Frank. To do that, I have got to crush it at its source."

Garland gestured impatiently. "Then you've got to change Mark Hardin—and people like him."

"I mean to try to do that, Frank," Caleb Kingman replied quietly. He leaned forward and took a sheet of yellow flimsy from his desk. "Yancy Donovan brought that out to me from town an hour ago. That is the reason that K will not ride just yet." It was a hand written telegram which said tersely:

> Senator Mark Hardin will arrive Fort Duncan 12th inst. Extend every courtesy.

For a moment, Frank Garland stared at the sheet; then pushed it away and returned his attention to the major.

"The twelfth is tomorrow, sir," he said softly. "You mean to have a showdown with Mark Hardin?"

"I do."

"You know what that can mean, sir."

"I know that, too," Major Kingman answered. "It does not matter. I do not intend that more people shall die out here to satisfy Mark Hardin's ambitions."

Garland reached for his hat, stood up slowly so that the lamplight shone across the brown planes of his face. There was admiration and warmth in his eyes as he looked down.

"You are a brave man, sir," he said softly. "K will be ready to ride when you give the word."

He saluted and passed on out into the other room. He paused surprised; Janet Davenport stood beside the lamp, her face white and strained as she stared at him.

"I heard what was said in there," she whispered so low that Frank scarcely heard. "Talk. Just talk! Does Gil's danger mean nothing at all to you, Captain Garland?"

Frank Garland looked at her for a long moment. Then

he said, "First things first, Miss Davenport. We will try to get to Lieutenant Hardin as soon as we can."

"But it is your fault that this has happened," she said then, her voice shaking a little. "Do you deny that?"

Garland inclined his head a little toward her, then moved to the door. "I deny nothing," he said. "Good night, Miss Davenport."

7. A Freighter, Called Pete

THE BUGLER at the main gate was sounding Tattoo as Frank Garland stepped out into the night. The wind, coming out of the north, was cold against his face now. That could be bad if K was to ride soon for, at this season of the year, anything could happen in this country of unpredictable weather. He shrugged that worry away. A man had no business borrowing trouble.

Light showed in a window of Oglethorpe Henderson's quarters and he debated as to whether or not he'd stop for a moment. Thorpe Henderson took the decision away from him then for the door opened and Henderson's voice called, "Frank? Thought that I recognized your step. Will you come in for a cup of coffee with us?"

For a moment Garland hesitated. It would be pleasant to spend a little time in talk with Thorpe and Mary Henderson. Then he remembered that he still had a chore to do tonight in Hagar.

"Sorry," he said. "I can't. I've got a little job yet to do tonight." He paused for a moment, then added soberly, "Major Kingman will hold services for Benson and Jarvis at ten tomorrow, Thorpe. K will be escort, of course. We'd like it if you'd ride with us."

"I'll be there," Oglethorpe Henderson said, his voice taking on a deeper note. "I heard what happened—a bad business, Frank. I thought that K—maybe all four companies of the garrison—would be riding out tomorrow. I'm wrong?"

"No one rides yet," Garland told him evenly. "The Old Man will tell you about it in the morning."

Mary Henderson came to stand beside her husband in the warm light that streamed from the door. A tall girl and

59

too thin, hating this country out here but not willing that her man should suffer it alone. There was a faint gladness in her voice as she greeted Frank Garland and he knew that she had heard him say that the garrison wasn't riding.

"What will the Indians do with Gil, Frank?" she asked.

"Nothing, probably," he said. He knew that was a lie, but it was not good to worry Mary unnecessarily when Thorpe might be going out with the column again soon. "The major thinks that Broken Feather and his band have left the reservation in protest against a rumored land steal. If that's so, they'll likely hold Gil to bargain with."

The light fell across the girl's plain face as she moved closer to her husband. "I am sorry for Miss Davenport," she said softly. "It is a terrible thing to believe that you have lost your man out here, Frank."

Garland nodded for he knew what she was thinking. It was three months ago when K had ridden back into Fort Duncan with Oglethorpe Henderson slung in a blanket between two mules and with a slug through him, too close. An Indian, drunk on Arco Blaine's whiskey, had done that, Garland thought grimly.

Thorpe Henderson was saying again, "Sure that you can't take a minute for a cup of coffee, Frank? Mary's got it hot."

"Thanks, Thorpe, another time. Will you get word to Jim Bestwood that K doesn't ride tomorrow? I may not see him again tonight. I'm going on into Hagar."

Garland went on down the packed walk. Nice people, he was thinking. Good people who made the best of life as it came to them—and who made life a little better for those who served with them.

His own quarters were beyond and there was no light waiting for him here, he thought with a little stab of loneliness. He pushed the door open and went in. Some of the day's closeness still lingered, unpleasant after the tang of outdoors, and it irritated him a little. He fumbled for the lamp, got it alight, and the yellow glow flooded across the room.

For a moment he stood looking with a faint distaste at

the littered table and the gear piled in one corner. Suddenly and without his willing it so, he wondered how Janet Davenport would look standing there in the doorway and gazing in. He laughed the idea harshly away.

Janet Davenport was not made for this country out here. She was meant for the soft lights of a drawing room, the faint music of hidden violins, and the murmur of polite conversation. She had nothing to do with the stark realities of Fort Duncan. With a battered patrol coming in and with two men roped across their saddles. Or with K ready to ride soon again.

Well, no matter.

Garland's belted gun hung from a hook on the wall and he took it down now; checked the loads and strapped it in its accustomed place against his leg. It felt good there, he reflected sardonically. It was a companion which had ridden with him for a long time now and one that he trusted well. He glanced sourly at the disordered room once more, then turned out the light and went back into the evening.

The barracks were quieter as he turned the corner and went on through the starlight to the stables beyond. Corporal McNair, who had been waiting in the shadows, stepped out into the uncertain light and saluted.

"I sort of took the liberty of saddlin' the cap'n's bay, sorr. You want me to lead him out?"

That surprised Frank Garland a little; then he remembered that McNair had been in the wagon when he had encountered Arco Blaine that afternoon and he nodded. "Thanks, corporal," he said. "You needn't have bothered."

"No bother, sorr." McNair disappeared into the shadows and returned leading the tall rawboned horse. He stood back while Garland mounted. "I wish the cap'n luck, sorr."

Garland lifted a hand and swung away.

The sentry on No. 1 challenged then called, "Pass, sir," and Garland rode on through the gate at a walk. Once beyond the Fort, he put the bay into a jogging trot and moved on toward where Hagar threw its smear of light across the prairie.

A coyote lifted its mournful song from the buttes to the northwest and the wind was still freshening, carrying more solidly now that hint of a storm on its breath. A faint depression settled over him as he rode. A lonesomeness which was born of the cold starlight and the memory of Benson and Jarvis and the thought of Major Kingman who was coming now to the end of his road.

For Frank Garland had no doubt as to what would happen when the major met Senator Mark Hardin and faced him down. The major would win temporarily for he would have Gil as a lever—a hostage, almost—if Gil wasn't already dead. But, in the end, he would lose for he was a man who had scorned influence through the long years of his service and he could not stand against the power which Mark Hardin would eventually bring.

And the end was inevitable. At the worst, a court-martial and dismissal in disgrace; at the best, retirement to live the rest of his life out in some obscure place, a shawl across his knees and nothing but his memories to sustain him. And all his work would have accomplished nothing. The Indians would go and the Indian lands would go and no one would remember that Caleb Kingman had tried to save them. No one except Marjory.

And Captain Frank Garland?

He didn't know. The years would likely march on in their plodding, remorseless way and, when they ended, the page would show nothing on the credit side except a thousand miles of dusty trail ridden; a few forgotten fights. Poker hands played and a few drinks taken—and nothing more.

For a moment, he thought of Janet Davenport and again he felt the faint stirring which had been there when he had looked down at her yesterday in the train's littered coach. A lovely woman—and afraid of something out here. And now that Gil Hardin was gone, she would go, too. Back to that shadowy land beyond the frontier's curtain which he, Frank Garland, no longer knew.

The trail dipped into a little swale and then the bay breasted the rise and Hagar lay sprawling in front of them a quarter of a mile away. Garland pulled the horse down to a walk and rode slowly into the main street of the town, the thoughts which had gnawed at him put away now and his mind wary again. His perceptions reached out to gather in the night-feel of the town; probed for any danger which the night might hide.

At the Deerfoot saloon, Garland dismounted, tied his horse and went on toward the swinging doors. Sounds came to his ears—the sounds of a hundred places like this scattered in a hundred towns. Nothing different here. Nothing new. The restless murmur of men's voices as they took their drinks and the clink of chips as they spent their money.

He pushed on in; stood for a moment just inside while his eyes adjusted themselves to the brightness of the swinging lamps. Men at the bar; men at the three poker tables at the room's far end. He laid his hard attention on the scene for a brief moment; then took his stand at the bar near the door. Arco Blaine was not there. Neither was the breed, Whitewater Charley. Finn, the chunky bartender, came presently.

"Evenin', captain," he said. "What's your pleasure? Come into town for a little fling tonight?"

"No," Garland said shortly. "I'm looking for Arco Blaine. Have you seen him?"

He saw Finn's eyes change and he knew that Arco had been here; knew, too, that he would find out nothing from Finn. The Army was not popular here in Hagar.

"Can't say as I have, captain." Finn polished at the bar with a rag. "People goin'—coming all the time. A man don't notice."

"Let it go," Garland told him. "Bring me a bottle and a glass, Finn."

The bartender set them out beside him, picked up Garland's money and moved away. Frank took his drink, watching the crowd behind him in the mirror behind the bar.

A freighter with the marks of the trail still on his clothes moved down the bar and peered drunkenly at Garland. A

63

big man, taller than Frank; heavier through the shoulders. Belligerence showed in his flushed face and Garland grew quietly watchful.

"You're the Army, huh?" the man demanded.

"That's right," Garland told him, turning his empty glass around in his fingers. He saw that Finn was watching from a distance. "What can I do for you, friend?"

The freighter's face got redder. "You ain't no friend of mine, Army!" he yelled hoarsely. Crazy drunk, Garland thought, and waited. The freighter reached a hand to steady himself against the bar. "Didn't see none of you damn yellow-legs around when the Injuns jumped us over by Red Butte last week! Where were you, Army? That's what I want to know!"

Garland didn't answer that. It would serve no purpose to tell this man that Red Butte was Indian country; that freight trains had no business being in there and that, if they got hurt when they did go, nobody could do much about it. The freighter pushed closer and others along the bar were beginning to turn and listen now. Garland could feel the unfriendliness building up like a tangible thing in the smoky light of the room.

"Hey, Army?" the freighter said again. "Where were you then? Paradin' your soldiers up an' down in their pretty little drills at Fort Duncan, hey? You think that is what we pay you for, Army?"

"You pay me for nothing," Garland told him roughly.

The freighter teetered on his feet, his eyes red and angry. "An' that's more than you're worth!" he yelled, lifting his voice so that it carried through the big room. "You yellow-legs ain't even got the guts to round up fellers like this here Arco Blaine who peddles whiskey and guns to the Injuns. You scared of him, too, Army?"

Garland said, letting his own voice carry now, "I think that you talk too much, friend. Go on home and sleep it off," and turned back to his drink.

The freighter stood for a moment, his face settling into puzzled and stupid lines. Then he lurched forward again, mumbling, "You don't turn your back on Pete Murphy,

Army," and grabbed for Garland's shoulder; half turned him back.

Anger ran swiftly through Frank Garland then, the violence which had been building steadily in him ever since he had seen K's scout come up out of Cache Creek with two men tied across their saddles. He stepped back a little.

"Take your hands off me," he said, his voice dangerous. "Keep them off."

The freighter stood for a moment, head down and peering at Garland from beneath his shaggy brows. Then he said, "I hate soldiers!" and rushed.

Garland slapped him with an open palm—a hard, full armed blow—and the man tottered on his heels for a moment; then growled deep in his throat and came on again. This time Frank hit him solidly in the stomach—damn the man, he was asking for this—and the freighter grunted and sat down on the floor, both hands held against his belly while he stared up.

The crowd at the bar moved restlessly and Garland turned a little so that he could lay the weight of his stare onto them. "Any of the rest of you want a part in this?"

Tension hung over the room for a long moment. Then a man said at the back of the crowd, "That damn Pete ain't got no sense when he's liquored. I don't want any part of nothin'."

The man nearest Frank waved a hand suddenly; drawled, "I reckon that goes for me, too." and turned away, calling for a drink.

The freighter was getting back to his feet. The belligerence had gone out of his eyes now and he swayed unsteadily for a moment. Garland caught him by the elbow, pulled him to the bar and poured a glass of whiskey for him. The freighter gulped it down and let his mouth go loose in a slow grin.

"I talk too much, Army," he said. "Feel like a mule had kicked me. No hard feelings?"

Garland stared at him for a moment; then his own mouth relaxed. "No hard feelings. What do you know about Arco Blaine, mister?"

"Just call me, Pete, Army," the freighter said. "We got jumped by a war party at Red Butte. When we got back to Esperance I heard it said that this feller, Blaine, was the one who was gettin' the Injuns stirred up. Sellin' 'em guns and whiskey. Like I said, I talk too much."

"Maybe not. You know where Arco Blaine is now?"

"He was in here drinkin' a couple of hours ago when I went out to eat," Pete said. "I don't like fellers who sell hootch and guns to the Injuns. Sure there ain't no hard feelings, Army?"

"No hard feelings," Garland told him again absently. He turned and called sharply, "Finn!"

The fat bartender came, his face a little worried now, and Garland paid for the drinks. "Finn," he said, "Arco Blaine was in here earlier. Where did he go?"

The bartender spread his hands and an aggrieved look crawled across his face. "I don't want to get mixed up in none of this business," Finn said halfheartedly. "I just mind my own."

"You're mixed up in this business already, Finn," Garland told him roughly. "Where'd Arco go?"

"Whitewater Charley sent word for him to come to the hotel," Finn mumbled. "Blaine left. That's all I know, captain."

"How long ago?"

"Maybe an hour. I didn't pay no attention."

Garland stared at him, hands flat on the bar. "All right," he said finally. "That's what I wanted to know."

Outside a front window of the Deerfoot, Corporal Tim O'Garragh slid his gun back into its holster and stepped deeper into the shadows. Things had been a little tight in there for a moment, he was thinking. Looked as though Frank Garland might have needed some help. But then the captain wasn't a man who needed help often.

At the rear of the saloon, the breed—Whitewater Charley—left another window and scuttled through the alley in the direction of the hotel. The instinct of self-preservation was strong in Whitewater Charley and he had seen

66

enough to know that he didn't want to face Captain Frank Garland tonight—or any other night. He'd just get his war bag out of Arco Blaine's room at the hotel and head for the hills.

8. Ambush in Hagar

ARCO BLAINE sat slumped at the rickety table in the room in the hotel in Hagar, an empty bottle in front of him. He had sent Whitewater Charley out for more whiskey and a thread of anger began to grow in him as the minutes went by and the breed had not yet returned.

It was fifteen minutes later when steps finally came pounding along the corridor outside and Blaine swung around a little in his chair, his eyes watchful as he dropped a hand to the gun at his hip and waited. Then the door slammed back and Whitewater Charley came in, his eyes scared as they darted around the room. He had brought no whiskey, Arco Blaine noted angrily.

"What's spooked you up?" he demanded harshly. "And where's the whiskey?"

The breed shook his head dumbly; then found his tongue. "Frank Garland's in the Deerfoot," he said in a thick voice. Askin' for you. Finn told him you was up here. He'll be coming along in a minute an' I ain't going to be here when he does!"

Arco Blaine lunged to his feet, his eyes hardening as he stared back at the breed. "You're not going anywhere," he said. "I'm not letting you run around loose, Charley—maybe to go out to the fort and spill all that you know about where Feather is holding Gil Hardin."

Whitewater Charley's swarthy face got a shade lighter as he edged a little toward the door. "I ain't no hero, Arco," he said thickly. "You know I wouldn't go near the fort."

"I'm going to see to it that you don't," Blaine retorted roughly. "Keep ahead of me, Charley, and don't try any tricks. I'd hate to have to go back to Esperance and tell your squaw that you died in the line of duty."

Sad resignation came into the breed's face and he shrugged his heavy shoulders. "What we going to do, Arco?"

"Look for Frank Garland," Blaine said, his eyes hard and flat. "And we'll look for him where he's not expecting us to be."

The two men pushed out into the dim corridor, Whitewater Charley in the lead and Blaine, his face thinned out and sober now, catfooting it along behind him. A door opened here to an outside stairs which led down to the back of the hotel. There was a woodpile and, beyond that, a stable and the bars of a corral. A dog barked suddenly and Blaine swore at him in a muffled voice and the barking stopped.

They skirted the corral and went across a back lot littered with cans and broken packing cases and then turned into an alley between Mahan's store and the barber shop. Charley shivered a little, hunching his shoulders against the wind.

Arco Blaine dropped a warning hand on his arm and the two edged forward toward the street. There was a pile of hides here, odorous in the night, and Blaine crouched behind them, hauling Whitewater Charley with him while he reconnoitered the street with his eyes.

Footsteps came scraping along the board sidewalk and a slouched, lurching figure passed by, dimly silhouetted against the starlight. Someone of the town going home to the comfort of his bed and his wife, Arco Blaine thought sardonically. He waited until the sound of the footsteps had died away and the street was empty again.

Then he said, keeping his mouth close to Whitewater Charley's ear, "Likely Garland left his horse at the Deerfoot and walked to the hotel. If I know him, he's there now and he'll have to come back by here to get to the Deerfoot again."

"I don't like this," Charley mumbled under his breath. "Suppose he don't? Suppose he takes it into his head to sneak around back the same as we done?"

"Damn it," Blaine snarled, "I don't care what you suppose. You just wait here for him to come by. I'll be across the street. One of us will get a shot at him no matter which way he comes!"

He waited a minute longer, his eyes probing the uncertain starlight of the dark street. Then he slid the gun from its holster at his hip and padded softly out across the dusty street. Presently the shadows swallowed him.

Whitewater Charley shivered a little as he crouched behind the pile of smelly hides. He pulled his coat closer about his shoulders and pinched himself deeper into the angle which the piled hides made against the wall of Mahan's store—oblivious to the sickening stench. From the direction of the Deerfoot, a man yelled—a long, shrill, "Whoooooeeee!" which echoed in the starlight; from still further away, the tinkle of a piano made a faint discord in the night.

Then Whitewater Charley tightened suddenly for there was a darker shadow out there in Hagar's street now. The shadow of a man, vague in the uncertain light, who moved steadily along. And he knew that that erect figure belonged to Frank Garland. He got slowly to his feet, drawing his gun and resting it along the top of the pile of hides.

Then Corporal O'Garragh's voice said softly behind him, "I wouldn't do that, Charley," and a sudden icy fear ran through the breed. His finger tightened spasmodically on the trigger and the roar of the gun filled the little alley and he knew vaguely that there was an answering streak of orange flame across the street. Then something— brutally heavy—struck against his temple, exploding the night into a galaxy of wheeling constellations and Whitewater Charley knew nothing more.

The cool air of the night tasted like good wine to Frank Garland as he came out of the Deerfoot and he stood for a moment, tasting it and letting it blow the stale smoke out of his nostrils. Then he turned slowly in the direction of the hotel. The smell of dust was suddenly more fresh on the wind now and as he tasted it his perceptions sharpened. A man had been moving in the street ahead of him, he

70

thought; powdering the dust beneath his boots so that it came down on the wind. He slowed his pace a little as he came abreast of the barber shop; tightened his scrutiny of the shadows.

Then a round yellow flower blossomed over there from the mouth of an alley and the racket of a shot ripped into the night. He whirled, dropping to one knee as his own gun came into his hand. A second shot, following fast on the heels of the first, whipped out at him from the opposite side of the street and, in its flash, he caught a faint glimpse of a crouching figure there.

He threw two bullets into the shadows as the night clamped down again; then sprinted for the shelter of Mahan's store, crouching low as he ran and expecting the slam of a bullet. A gun hammered three times from the alley, a dozen yards away, where the first shot had come from and Garland heard the *whuck* of the bullets as they struck the wooden front of the building across the street. A man swore over there—Blaine's voice, Garland thought—and then there was a scrape of boot heels against boards and the night was quiet once more.

After a little, Corporal O'Garragh's voice called softly, "Captain, you all right?" and Garland relaxed, knowing that the last of the firing had been O'Garragh's.

"I'm all right," he grunted. "I think that's Blaine across the street."

"It's Blaine all right," O'Garragh called back. "I got the breed here." Then he added, as the muffled sound of a horse's running drifted from beyond the buildings across the street, "Arco's pulled foot, I reckon."

Men were streaming out of the Deerfoot fifty yards away and others were crowding out of the hotel. Garland straightened; automatically he fed fresh loads into his gun and slid it back into the holster. O'Garragh was coming out from behind the pile of hides.

"What are you doing here?" Garland asked roughly, tension flowing out of him with a welcome relief. "Did you fire that first shot?"

71

O'Garragh, his shoulders bulky against the starlight, moved out into the street. "Whitewater Charley fired it," he said laconically. "I had a gun in his ribs—guess I scared his trigger finger."

"Just as well for me," Garland grunted. "He spoiled Arco's shot. Where is the breed?"

"Layin' in the alley with a headache," O'Garragh said, satisfaction in his voice. "I laid the barrel of my gun against his head good."

A man, running hard down the street, called hoarsely, "What is it? Who's been shot?" Garland caught him by the arm and turned him roughly around.

"Go on back to the Deerfoot and have a drink, friend," he said evenly. "Nobody's been shot."

For a moment the man stood there, gaping stupidly; then he turned and went slowly back. Garland saw the others pause, then drift back, too. He swung back to Corporal O'Garragh.

"What the devil are you doing in Hagar at this time of night, Tim?" he asked roughly and knew the answer even before he had asked the question. There was not enough light here in the street for him to see O'Garragh's slow grin but he knew it was there.

"Seein' the sights, captain," O'Garragh said with a hint of a brogue running in his voice. "I'm told that they're nice in Hagar at this time of year."

"I ought to slam you in the guardhouse," Garland growled, warmth running through him as he looked at O'Garragh. "I'm obliged to you, Tim. Let's get White-water Charley. That lad goes back to Duncan with us to-night."

Taps had long since gone as they answered the sentry's challenge at the main gate and moved on across the parade ground to halt at last in front of the small guard room. Sergeant Mickeljon, of K, was sergeant of the guard. He came out, buckling his belt as he came, and stopped, his eyes curious as the corporal of the guard held a lantern so that its light fell across the little group. Whitewater

Charlie, still unconscious, was slung over O'Garragh's saddle.

"Got a prisoner for you, sergeant," Garland said crisply. "The breed, Whitewater Charley. Lock him up and give him whatever attention he needs. He's not hurt bad."

Sergeant Mickeljon said, "Yes, sir. We'll take care of him."

"See that you hang onto him," Garland said thinly. "I'll talk to him tomorrow."

The sergeant said, "Yes, sir," again and Corporal O'Garragh swung back into his saddle. The two men rode silently until they were opposite Garland's quarters. Then O'Garragh said, "I'll take the captain's horse to the stables." Garland nodded.

"Thanks, O'Garragh," he said softly. "For that business back there in Hagar, too. Good night."

"Good night, sir." O'Garragh took the reins and lead the bay behind him.

That was what he liked about Captain Garland, he was thinking. No fuss over what had been done. No sentimentality. No blather. No nothing. Just: "Thanks, O'Garragh." You could cotton to a man like that.

9. The Girl From Suds Row

K COMPANY was drawn up—mounted and with sabers at the carry and chin straps of dress helmets tight against weather-beaten cheeks—as the wagon with its two flag-draped boxes rolled slowly toward the main gate and passed on through on its way to the cemetery beyond. Frank Garland sang out a curt command and the line of K melted and swung into a column of fours and followed, the horses bobbing their heads and snorting in the dust.

A little knot of people had gathered at the forlorn acre where Fort Duncan buried its dead as Garland swung the company into line again. Marjory Kingman was there, her face composed beneath the dark bonnet—ten years out of style—which hid her graying hair. Janet Davenport was beside her and that surprised Frank for he had not expected it. Other officers, sidearms at their belts, waited with their wives standing silently beside them; farther along, the noncommissioned officers stood quietly with their women.

For this was a family sorrow. A grief to be borne by all and a duty not to be slighted.

Here, in this harsh land, a man had few rewards and it was right that—when his time came to him—his friends should be here to honor him as best they might. Private or colonel—it made no difference, for the same dust came eventually to fill the mouths of all. He donned the shoddy blue that the Army gave him; took the meager pay and ate the mouldy beans; breathed the scorching dust of the sun-blistered trails and shivered in the dampness of the cheerless dawns and came finally to his six feet of earth like this.

Why did a man do it? Benson, Jarvis—any man?

Patriotism? Not likely for that was a vague and

grandiose word which would have meant little to Benson or Jarvis. A word for the mouths of orators or politicians. An ephemeral word, having little connection with the everyday business of soldiering. Or dying.

Ambition?

Hardly, for the Army demanded much and gave little in return, Frank Garland thought dourly. There was Major Caleb Kingman with his years of service rewarded only by the old wounds which bothered him on a cold morning—Major Kingman whom a politician's greed would presently break. And there was Jim Bestwood with the good years of his life behind him now and nothing but a genteel poverty on a niggardly pension lying ahead for him. No, not ambition.

Laziness, the wish for adventure, the vague seeking of a security of a sort? Those could be the things which had brought them here perhaps. Frank Garland didn't know.

Perhaps it did not really matter, he thought now what counted was that they had volunteered themselves for their own reasons and in their own manner to do a tough and thankless job. And they had deserved a better fate than to die on the banks of some little-known river because some young fool had lost his head or had been afraid or had gotten the glory light in his eyes.

Major Kingman's voice drew Garland's attention back to the scene in front of him. A somber scene against a sorrowing sky.

". . . he leadeth me beside the still waters. . . ."

Major Kingman's voice died away and he closed the Book in his hands and bent his head for a moment. Then the volleys cracked out their farewell, and Trooper Monk Walters' trumpet lent its clear, liquid notes to the morning and the brief ceremony was done.

Garland put the company into column again and they went back at the trot, the troopers consciously shaking solemnity from their shoulders for this was just a detail in the day's work. There would be other funeral parades in the days to come as there had been other funeral parades in the days past.

Corporal O'Garragh said to Monk Walters, riding beside him, "That's the way it goes, Monk. One day you're here—the next, you're nothing but a line drawn through the morning report."

Monk Walters rocked a little in his saddle and whistled a few bars of "Garry Owen" between his teeth. Then he said, breaking the tune in the middle of a bar, "Don't worry none about me, Corporal O'Garragh, sir. I'm indestructible. I'll live forever. Nothing happens to Trumpeter Walters, sir."

O'Garragh grunted. "Jarvis thought that," he said.

First Sergeant Jim Bestwood called from the flank of the column, "Cut out that damned talking," and they went on in silence with the yellow dust exploding in little spurts from beneath the shod hoofs of the horses.

The sky hung in a slate gray roof overhead and the wind was cold. Just another day's chore. Tomorrow would be another day and tomorrow would bring other chores.

The little groups in the cemetery broke up slowly, began to drift away. Officers helped their ladies into the waiting wagons which had brought them there, mounted their horses, and moved alongside as the wagons turned back toward the gate. Major Kingman, his face more tired than she had seen it before, came to offer Janet Davenport his arm but she shook her head.

"I should like to walk back, major," she said soberly. "It is not too far. Do you mind?"

He considered that for a moment, his eyes studying her, and she could feel the refusal forming in him. This was not Fifth Avenue; this was Fort Duncan, in Dakota Territory, and no place for young women to walk unescorted.

"Please. There are things that I need to think about, major. By myself."

"If you wish, Janet," he said in a gentle voice. "Do not get beyond the sight of the sentry at the main gate. These are troubled times here now. I wouldn't want you hurt."

"I will be careful," she answered, her tone so low that he scarcely heard.

Major Kingman gave her a swift look from eyes which did not wholly conceal his worry. "You must not take all of this too hard, Janet," he said and she knew that he was speaking now of the two men who had been lowered into the earth such a short while ago. Then he shook his head and added, "And you must try not to worry about Gilbert. He'll be all right—and we'll get him back for you soon."

"It is not about Gilbert that I need to think right now, major. It's about some other things which I'm afraid I never considered much before."

Major Kingman nodded. "I understand," he said and went on to where his wife waited.

The wagon moved on off and Janet stood for a moment, watching it go, and then turned her sober attention back to the land about her. Hagar was a smudged scar on the prairie two miles away, its smokes rising in a gray pall. To the right, a ragged line of alder and willow and cottonwood showed where Cache Creek ran. And beyond were the dun foothills, lifting toward that raw, tangled country where Gil had lost his freedom and two men had lost their lives. She turned away, awed and a little frightened.

This country was so impersonal. So exacting, so cruel. And yet men faced it, unafraid, and bent it to their will. The thought gave her a sudden small thrill of pride and she found herself trying to remember the faces of those men in K Company—impassive against the gray sky as they had sat their horses there facing her.

And, of those faces, that of Frank Garland stood out with the greatest clarity in her mind. For, against her will, she had been studying it and only half hearing the words which Major Kingman had been speaking. A strong face, she had thought; hard and with a hint of ruthlessness in it. But there was kindness there, too, and the promise of humor. And sadness; she had seen that yesterday when he had met her on the train. She wondered from what that sadness had sprung; it had not been a little thing, she knew.

Now, as she turned slowly, she saw that another still lingered here in the cemetery with her. A girl—little more than a child, almost—with yellow hair blowing about her face as she looked out across the lifeless wasteland.

It was Annie Helfron and she held a small bunch of late wild flowers in her hands. As Janet watched, she moved forward slowly to place them on one of the new graves; stood, looking down with an expressionless face.

There was a proudness in that girl standing there in her cheap calico dress, Janet thought suddenly. Something strong and fierce and indomitable. That same indefinable thing which had been in Frank Garland's face—in Major Kingman's, in Marjory's. The mark of a brotherhood; the badge of those who served and took pride in their serving.

It was a thing to be earned; not a thing given. She knew, all at once and with a startling clarity, that Gil had never belonged in that brotherhood, and she had known this all along but had turned her face from it.

And now it was too late, for she had come here to marry Gil and Gil would return. It was the Gils of the world who always returned, though others died that they might.

Impulsively she started for where Annie Helfron was still standing; stopped uncertainly as she saw the other girl turn and come toward her, instead. Annie stopped a few feet away; stood studying Janet's face with grave eyes.

"You are Miss Davenport, aren't you?" she asked finally and Janet nodded her head.

"Yes," Janet answered in a low voice. The steadiness of the other girl's eyes disconcerted her a little for she thought that she could see the hint of a faint accusation there. She went on a little hurriedly. "One of these soldiers was—special to you?"

"Yes, Miss Davenport. Georgie Jarvis. He was special. Not like you think, maybe. Like a brother, I guess."

Annie's voice was steady, devoid of emotion, but Janet saw the swift pain that flowed through her eyes. So very young, Janet thought with swift pity. A child—yet with a woman's capacity for grief and a woman's capacity for pain.

She said in a low voice, "I am sorry. Terribly sorry. Will you tell me your name?"

"Annie," the girl said. Then added without embarrassment; without rancor, "Annie Helfron from Suds Row, Miss Davenport. I—I must go now."

"Not yet," Janet cried. She had to understand the things which lay behind Annie Helfron's eyes and now she flung a hand toward where the bunch of wild flowers lay. "Tell me about him, Annie. What was he like? What did he think? You said that he was like a brother——"

Her voice trailed away and she knew that she was making a fool of herself. Creating a scene in front of this homely little girl standing there with the wind whipping at her calico dress. But it didn't matter. She had to find out.

Annie was looking at her soberly. "There's nothing to tell, Miss Davenport," she said with a faint wonder in her voice. "Georgie Jarvis was a soldier. He took a soldier's death. You understand such things when you are a soldier's daughter." And then she added softly, looking directly at Janet again, "Or a soldier's wife."

Janet turned away, with a quick shame—how she had complained yesterday because Gil had not been at the train to meet her! Petty—how petty! She seemed to see again the way that the driver's shoulders had stiffened at her protest to Frank Garland. She could hear the faint scorn in Corporal McNair's voice as he had said, "Hup, Bess! Get along, you brokendown dead beat!" And Georgie Jarvis had been dead.

Then she remembered something more.

It was a snatch of conversation which she had overheard as the major's orderly had gossiped with the wagon driver while they waited outside her window that morning. At first she had paid no attention. Then she had heard Gil's name mentioned and had moved closer to listen.

"The lieutenant led Brecheen an' the rest into a trap, the way I heard it," the orderly was saying. "Just piled right in wavin' his saber until the Injuns grabbed him. That's a glory-huntin' officer for you, Jase. His father's a big shot in Washington, so I hear."

"That ain't buying Benson and Jarvis anything," the other man had answered and Janet had been able to feel the scorn in his words. "All the glory that they're gettin' is the horn blowed over them this morning. That ain't much in my book."

Janet's face flushed a little now as she remembered that. She had been angry and sure that they had lied. But now she was not sure at all.

"There is so much about this land that I don't understand," she said. "I had thought that things would be so different."

Annie stood there, the wind whipping her thin dress about her legs while she studied that. Then she said gravely, "Things are the way that they've got to be, I guess, Miss Davenport. I am sorry that Lieutenant Hardin was captured. Please don't worry—I know that Captain Garland —and K—will get him back."

The sympathy in the girl's voice was more than Janet could bear. "Why don't you say what you're really thinking?" she cried out wildly. "Why don't you tell me that it was all Gil Hardin's fault that those two men were buried this morning! That he killed them just as though he had pointed a gun at their heads!"

"Because it wouldn't be true, Miss Davenport," Annie said gently, moving a little closer. "Georgie Jarvis wouldn't have said that if he had come back. Everybody makes mistakes, even officers. You must not think that about Lieutenant Hardin."

Then Janet was suddenly crying and the younger woman's arm was about her waist and all at once she felt a little comforted. Presently they went back together across the dun prairie which led back to the main gate.

Whitewater Charley was sitting dejectedly on the rude guardhouse bunk as Frank Garland came in, followed by Toronto Peters. A lump, the size of a hen's egg, marred the side of his head. He kept his eyes on the dirt floor and he shifted his feet uneasily.

Garland demanded roughly, "Where's Blaine holed up, Charley? You've got no reason to hold out on us. He isn't going to help you now."

Whitewater Charley shook his head and looked up, a hopeless resignation settling into his face. "I don't know, cap'n," he said dully.

Toronto Peters, his gray-stubbled face screwed into a scowl, said, "Maybe you'd ought to let me talk to him out behind the stables, Frank. Maybe he'd remember some of the answers then."

Fear made a dull wash across Whitewater Charley's face —he knew Toronto Peters. "I swear to God, I don't know," he said. "I'd tell you if I did! I don't want nothing more to do with Arco Blaine! I wish I'd never seen him!"

"Where is he?" Garland asked remorselessly.

"He's probably took to the hills by now. He figured on makin' a deal for the officer that Feather captured up on the Blackbird."

"Now we're getting somewhere," Garland said. "Do you know where Feather is, Charley?"

"Yeah," Whitewater Charley said, his eyes suddenly becoming sly. "I know. Will you keep Arco Blaine away from me if I tell you that, cap'n?"

"We'll keep him away."

"Feather's holed up in a place the Injuns call Hole-that-Hides," Whitewater Charley said slowly. "It's a hell of a place to get into. Not many white men know about it."

"Can you guide a column there?"

"I know the way."

Frank Garland said, "Good! You'll have the chance, Charley," and wheeled away. Toronto Peters lingered.

"See that you don't forget where that place is, boy," he grunted. "Accident might happen to you, if you did."

The scout drew a forefinger in a suggestive circle around the top of Whitewater's scalp; then followed Garland on out, laughing softly as he went.

10. Letter From Arco Blaine

JANET DAVENPORT and Annie Helfron came slowly back to the main gate. The sentry on No. 1 post watched them covertly from the corners of his eyes but saying nothing. He was glad that they had come in—the major had told him to watch out for them and that was an extra chore. He dismissed the matter from his mind and went back to his pacing again—he hated guard duty. Thirty steps out and thirty steps back. One-two-three-four. One-two-three-four. . . . His hitch would be up next month and he'd take his pay and get out of this condemned country. Go to St. Louis, maybe; or maybe even to New York. He'd never been there and he'd heard that a man could have himself a time.

The corporal of the guard came out onto the narrow porch and stared sourly after the two girls who had just passed; clicked his tongue against his teeth with a faint irritation. Then he turned his attention onto the sentry on Post No. 1. Hitched at his belt and spat.

"Stop ogling them girls, soldier," he said sourly. "You ain't out here just to see the sights."

He turned smartly and went on back into the guardhouse and the sentry on No. 1 mumbled under his breath, "Smart, ain't you, you fat Mick," and went on with his pacing. One-two-three-four. The devil with the Army, he was thinking, and the devil with Corporal Murtaugh. He'd like to . . .

His name was Private Fleigheimer—thirty-seven years old—and he rode in Tim O'Garragh's squad and Corporal O'Garragh did not consider him a good soldier. He had taken the back of his hand to him on occasion. O'Garragh was a hard man.

Annie Helfron paused—she and Janet had walked in silence since they had left the cemetery—and turned a little so that she faced the other girl. "Here is where I turn, Miss Davenport," she said slowly. "Good-by."

Impulsively, Janet reached out and placed her hand on Annie's arm. "Won't you call me Janet, Annie?" she asked urgently. "And I would like it if you would come and see me."

Annie Helfron shook her head in slow decision. "No, Miss Davenport," she answered. "When you have been longer on an Army post you will learn that Suds Row and Officers' Row don't mix. It has to be that way, I guess. I'm sorry about your man."

She wheeled suddenly and went off down the hard-packed path and Janet watched her go, not quite under-standing and a little hurt. Then, as she turned back, she was aware that two men had come out onto the porch of the guardhouse and that one of them was Frank Garland.

She realized with a faint warmth beginning to run through her, that he was coming toward her now. And why was that, she wondered. She had treated him badly last night; flung the blame for Gil's capture into his face. She should be turning away, showing him her disdain by going on toward where Major Kingman's quarters waited across the parade ground. Yet she didn't.

Frank Garland came up, moving without haste and with that easy freedom which she had remarked yesterday on the depot's platform. He had stopped and was touching his fingers to the brim of his hat, nodding a little and with his face grave.

"Miss Davenport," he said and there was neither excess cordiality nor excess reserve in his voice. It was, Janet thought with a little resentment, exactly the same tone in which he had addressed that corporal yesterday.

She said icily, "Good morning, Captain Garland. You had something to say to me?"

Frank Garland nodded, his gray eyes holding her against her will. "News of Gil, Miss Davenport. Not much—but a little. He is alive. We have reason to believe that the Indians are holding him at a place called Hole-that-Hides back in the hills. I thought you'd want to know."

"Thank you, captain." She was surprised that the news seemed to mean so little to her now. "It was kind of you to tell me. If you will excuse me—I must go now."

He looked at her for a long moment; then touched his hat brim again and said, "I understand. Good-by, Miss Davenport," and swung away toward the barracks.

For a moment Janet watched him go, biting a little at her lower lip. The ill-mannered boor, she thought angrily. He hadn't even offered to accompany her to the major's quarters; had left her standing foolishly here alone.

Gil would not have done that. Instinctively Gil would have told her the things that she wanted to hear—and not in the tone that he used to soldiers, either! Gil would not have . . .

And then the anger died suddenly in her as she turned blindly back along the path. She tried to remember Gil as she had seen him last—handsome and dashing and debonair in his new uniform. The little trick that he had of smiling with one corner of his mouth only and the smooth caress of his voice and the bold possession of his eyes. But another face kept pushing those things away.

Frank Garland's face.

Strength there where Gil had only prettiness—and she hated herself for thinking that. Decision and assurance and steadiness in the flat planes of his face and in the firm set of his mouth, where Gil had only a selfish wilfulness. That sadness which lurked at the back of Frank Garland's eyes. But Gil's eyes were arrogant and intolerant and they held the conceit which he had never made any attempt to hide from her.

She was almost running when she came again to Major Kingman's quarters. She paused on the porch to catch her breath. Mess call was sounding across the parade ground— the brassy, impudent notes of the bugle buffeting against the wind. Caleb Kingman's low voice drifted out to her through the window and, without really meaning to, Janet listened.

"Frank Garland and O'Garragh picked the half-breed, Whitewater Charley, up in Hagar last night," the major was saying. "He's known to be Arco Blaine's man. I think that there was trouble but Frank didn't say and I didn't ask him. Sometimes it's best not to pry too closely into these things, Maggie."

"What kind of trouble, Caleb?" Marjory Kingman asked.

"Blaine tried to ambush Frank, I think," the major answered slowly. "There was shooting—I learned that from Thorpe this morning. Anyway, it wasn't successful."

A cold hand suddenly squeezed at Janet's heart. She remembered the name—Arco Blaine—that was the man whom they had met yesterday afternoon while they were coming from Hagar. The one who had stared at her with that bold and faintly calculating smile.

"If there was any shooting you can be sure that Arco Blaine shot from behind," Marjory Kingman said with a swift thread of worry running through her voice. "That man is bad, Caleb."

"I know," Major Kingman answered heavily. "He's bitter and vengeful—he could be the key to this whole mess if we could only lay our hands on him."

"In what way?"

"With him in our hands we could probably effect Gil's release without more bloodshed. More than that, we would have enough evidence, I think, to crush this land grab when Senator Hardin gets here. With Gil free and Broken Feather on his way back to the reservation, there would be no need to send out the troops." The major stopped speaking for a long moment; then added with a faintly bitter note in his voice, "Until some new Mark Hardin and some new Arco Blaine came along, Maggie."

Marjory Kingman came to the door then; saw Janet and said swiftly, "My dear! What in the world are you doing out here in the wind? Come on in here before you catch your death!" and drew the girl on into the room's warmth.

Caleb Kingman was sitting in the deep chair by the fireplace and he stood up, a little slowly because of his weight, and bowed a little and smiled at her. She saw that his eyes were questioning but she didn't want to talk just now.

Marjory Kingman, seeming to understand, took her arm and together the two of them went on into the bedroom. Last night, Janet had thought Marjory Kingman nice but a little dowdy—definitely provincial. Why, she had wondered with a faint superiority then, did these Army women let themselves go so? The sun-parched skin; the clothes so long out of style.

But now she was beginning to understand better; to see things with clearer eyes. She was beginning to glimpse the courage and the fortitude which lay behind these women who had left ease and comfort and security to come out here—following their men to their appointed places—so that their man's home might follow, too. Would she, she wondered with a swift panic, be able now to stand beside Gil with the same strength and pride which ran through Marjory—through Annie Helfron?

She made up her mind with a sudden resolve as she faced the older woman. "Is it true that Gil behaved badly on that scout up the Blackbird, Mrs. Kingman? Please tell me," she added urgently. "I've got to know!"

She saw the swift caution which came into Marjory Kingman's eyes and understood it for what it was. The instinctive protection which walled the clan about when one of the family was in danger. Gil could be good or bad but the regiment would not condemn Gil to a stranger. Even to her.

"Gil was—is," Marjory Kingman said, correcting herself swiftly, "a young and impetuous officer, Janet. A little rash at times, perhaps—most young officers are. But he will learn. It is possible that he was too impetuous this time but we can't judge that while we sit here at home. We must wait."

Just words, Janet was thinking bitterly. And they answered nothing that she had to know.

"Was he a coward?"

The question wrenched itself out of her almost of its own volition and again she saw that intangible veil slide

86

across Marjory Kingman's eyes. But the older woman's voice was calm and untroubled as she answered.

"We have no cowards in this regiment, Janet," she answered. "This regiment does not tolerate cowards."

Janet sat slowly down on the bed; folded her hands in her lap. From beyond the small window, which opened on the parade ground, she heard the clatter of a horse's hoofs; the major's low voice as he spoke with someone out there. Marjory Kingman was looking down at her now with a faint compassion in her eyes.

"You must not take this too hard, Janet," she was saying, echoing the words which her husband had used out there in the cemetery earlier. "Everything will be all right. And Gil's father is arriving this afternoon. That will be better for you."

Suddenly Janet knew that she didn't want to see Mark Hardin—she was afraid of the man with his probing, relentless eyes and the craggy ruthlessness of his face. She wanted to think of something else; almost in desperation, she changed the subject.

"This man, Arco Blaine?" she asked slowly. "I overheard you and the major talking as I came———"

Her voice trailed away as she saw the spark of cold anger which was forming at the back of Marjory Kingman's eyes on the mention of Blaine's name. "I said that we had no cowards in this regiment, Janet," she answered softly. "I should have told you that once there was one. His name was Arco Blaine."

"He tried to kill Captain Garland?"

Marjory Kingman's lips tightened. "I had better tell you," she said. "It's not a pretty story. Three years ago, Company K was garrisoning a small outpost named Fort Corse. It's forty miles south of here. The company was away—in the field—and Arco Blaine had been left there with a few men to guard the post and the sick and the few women. He was a lieutenant in the regiment then."

Marjory Kingman stopped suddenly and turned toward the door but Janet came swiftly from the bed to put a hand on the older woman's arm.

"Frank Garland was there?" she asked. Her voice was little more than a whisper as she used his first name for the first time. "Tell me, please. I think that it's important."

"Frank was riding with the column a hundred miles away," Marjory Kingman replied tonelessly. "An Indian raiding party hit Fort Corse one night. Arco Blaine was drunk—so drunk that he wasn't fit to command. A sergeant major, named Hewlett got out of his sick bed and beat the raid off—before he was killed. Martha Garland, Frank's wife, was killed, too, Janet."

Marjory Kingman's voice trailed flatly away and Janet stood for a moment, her thoughts tangled while she stared at the faded curtains which hid the window. She said then, "Captain Frank Garland's wife," and Marjory Kingman nodded.

"Arco Blaine was court-martialed. Dismissed from the service. Now you know why he has tried to kill Frank."

"Frank's wife," Janet asked, "Was she very beautiful?"

"Yes," Marjory Kingman answered. "Very beautiful and Frank Garland was very much in love with her."

"It is the reason for the sadness in his eyes," Janet murmured and went back to sit on the edge of the bed again. For a moment longer, Marjory Kingman lingered. Then she went on out, closing the door softly behind her.

Alone in her room, Janet wrestled with her confused thoughts. She tried to picture what life would be like here with Gil. But his image was dim and uncertain now and she could remember only that evening when she had given him the promise that she would come. . . .

The Hudson had been silver in the moonlight and the band had been playing "Benny Havens" as the last hop had ended. And there had been Gil, straight and beautiful in his gray uniform with the brass buttons.

"It won't be very long," Gil had said to her that night. "A few short years on the frontier—then back to Washington and the Department. My father will arrange all that. You'll be the most beautiful woman in the Army, Jan."

It had been so easy to believe. She would come out to

him and they would be married as soon as he had settled in his new post in Dakota Territory and could send for her.

Dakota Territory! It had sounded romantic and glamorous and faraway. Different from the humdrum life of Connecticut. And she and Gil would be there, all by themselves and with no family to be saying always, "Do this. Do that." A high adventure, that was the way that it had seemed then.

There had been a few days in Washington when she had gone down to visit and to meet Gil's father, Mark Hardin, a domineering man whose eyes had frightened her a little. But that had been forgotten in the teas and the dances and the important people that she had met as the future daughter-in-law of Senator Mark Hardin. That had been nearly a year-and-a-half ago now.

At first Gil's letters had been gay and enthusiastic but, in the last few months, a disturbing note had crept into them. A rashness and a complaint—which had almost seemed like a whimper—that had disturbed her more and more.

The major, commanding at Fort Duncan, was an old fool and should have been retired long ago. A doddering old fogey who could rise no further in his profession; who had no use for young ideas; who wished to hold everyone else down to his own level. His captain was a martinet named Garland. Up from the ranks. A slave driver, uncouth, and little better than an enlisted man. Well, there would be ways of dealing with him. . . .

That was the way that Gil's letters had sounded, full of pettishness, cavilling. And in his veiled threats she had seemed to sense the same selfish ruthlessness in Gil which she had seen in his father's face during those few short days in Washington. The arrogance of position which led a man to trample down those beneath him who might stand in his way.

It had confused her, generating in her that vague fear which had been shadowed in her eyes and which Frank Garland had noted on the train. But a fear of what? She did not know.

She relaxed on the bed and closed her eyes. Across the parade ground the bugles were sounding First Call for afternoon drill, the brassy notes lifting and falling—fading on the wind. Presently she slept uneasily.

It was late afternoon when she awakened. For a moment she lay trying to recall where she was and what subtle disturbance had crept into her consciousness to awaken her. Then it came again; a faint but insistent tapping at the window of her room and she got up and went across to open it.

A lanky man, with a lined and sunburned face, was standing outside her window. He touched his hat with an apologetic gesture and held a folded note toward her.

"Yancy Donovan, ma'am," he said. "I was told to give this to you. If you want me I'll be at the sutler's store."

Automatically she took the slip and the man was gone, moving hastily away down the path. The paper was smudged and it bore a man's handwriting, boldly slanted.

Miss Davenport:
   If you wish to see Lieutenant Gilbert Hardin freed unharmed you will come to Hagar at once. Yancy Donovan will bring you. Destroy this note and keep its contents to yourself.
                                        Your servant,
                                           Arco Blaine.

For a moment Janet stood there staring at the writing. Her first reaction was anger at the man's effrontery in daring to suggest such a thing. Then her anger suddenly died away and the memory of what she had heard Major Caleb Kingman say earlier came to strike her like a blow.

"With Blaine in our hands we could probably effect Gil's release without more bloodshed . . . avert the thing that Mark Hardin is trying to do. . . ."

She made up her mind swiftly. It was Gil's headstrong wilfulness that had caused this thing. His father's schemes. Even she was not blameless. Now, she could do no less

90

than Annie Helfron, the major, or Marjory Kingman, or any of the rest would do.

She had no definite plan but she meant to go to Hagar. She meant to see Arco Blaine.

The front room was empty as she looked out of the door of her own room, hastily tying the strings of her bonnet beneath her chin. She listened for a moment and then moved swiftly to the front door; opened it and went on down the walk.

The note, forgotten, lay on the dresser behind her.

11. "K Marches Tomorrow"

FRANK GARLAND moved across the parade ground toward where the dozen other officers of the garrison were waiting for him on the porch of headquarters. They nodded greetings as he came up and then followed him as he went on inside. Andrews, who commanded I, and Babson of L and Whittaker of M. Their lieutenants and Smedley Weeks, the rotund contract surgeon.

A fire burned in a cast-iron stove at the back of the short hallway and the warmth was good after the bite of the air outside. Sergeant major Dolliver, a feisty little man with drooping mustaches, looked up from his desk which was across from the adjutant's office; frowned importantly as he saw the officers and went on back to his work. Corporal Greenbriar, the headquarters clerk, peered out curiously as the officers filed on by and the door of the adjutant's office closed behind them.

"What's the Old Man having an Officers' Call now for?" he wanted to know. He was a hollow-chested man of twenty-nine who liked to nose into things which were going on. "Two o'clock in the afternoon's a funny time for Officers' Call."

Sergeant major Dolliver knew that and it increased his irritation. Officers' Call was supposed to be at 11:45 in the morning—it said so in the list of calls, neatly printed out in Dolliver's own hand and tacked on the bulletin outside Dolliver's door.

He said sarcastically now, taking his displeasure out on Corporal Greenbriar, "I guess when the major wants some advice on how to run this post he'll probably ask you."

"Greenbriar's just the boy that could give it to him,

92

sarge," the corporal said flippantly. He elevated his feet to the top of the sergeant's desk and took a cigar from his pocket.

The sergeant major snorted. "Get those damn feet down off of my desk!"

Corporal Greenbriar complied slowly, squinting through the smoke of his cigar at the closed door of the adjutant's office. Muffled voices came from behind the panels but he couldn't make out what they were saying and that irked him; he liked to keep abreast of things that were going on.

"I'll bet that they're talking about what to do about Lieutenant Hardin," he said finally, scowling a little. "You know what I heard? I heard that the lieutenant went crazy. Just charged right down into——"

"Never mind what you heard," Sergeant major Dolliver snapped in a severe voice. "It is not a soldier's business to go around spreading rumors about his officers. I told you that before, Corporal Greenbriar."

"So you have," Greenbriar admitted blandly. "Now tell me something else. Tell me why nothing is being done about getting Lieutenant Hardin back, sarge. He's important, that one. His pappy swings a big stick back in Washington. Or didn't you know?"

Sergeant major Dolliver thought that over for a long moment, his thin lips pursed disapprovingly. He did not believe in gossiping about his officers but this time his own curiosity got the better of him. He, too, had wondered why the four companies of the garrison hadn't been ordered up the Blackbird at daybreak this morning. It was another of those things that bothered him.

"I know, all right," he grunted. He didn't, but he had no intention of admitting that to Corporal Greenbriar. "I know something else, too, but I don't know as I ought to tell you."

"I'm tight-mouthed as a clam," Greenbriar said, grinning encouragement. "Come on, sarge."

Dolliver scowled at him. "Senator Hardin is coming here on the evening train," he said finally. "So the major has waited to send the troops out until the senator gets here."

"Why would he want to do that?" Corporal Greenbriar asked, scowling as he fingered his chin.

"You ask too many questions," Sergeant major Dolliver said disgustedly. "How would I know what the major wanted to do? Quit bothering me so that I can get this report finished."

The clerk dropped the butt of his cigar into a brass spittoon; got lazily to his feet and reached for his hat. "I got to go over to K to see about their morning report, sarge," he said too casually. "It was all fouled up this morning again."

He went through the door and back along the hallway where he stoked the fire in the cast-iron stove. The major's voice came faintly to his ears from beyond the closed door of the office and he listened for a moment; then turned and went on out into the windy afternoon.

After he had gone, Sergeant major Dolliver scowled a little uneasily at the papers in front of him. He had talked too much, he was thinking. The major hadn't told him in so many words to keep quiet about the arrival of Senator Mark Hardin that afternoon. He had the feeling, though, that somehow the senator's arrival was going to mean trouble—a lot of trouble—and he should have had better sense than to go blathering the news around like an old woman!

That damned Greenbriar.

Lieutenant Henderson led the way into the major's office and said crisply, "All of the officers are present, sir." Major Kingman, behind his desk, nodded and motioned for Henderson to close the door which led into the hall.

"I have got certain things to tell you, gentlemen," Major Kingman began, weighing his words carefully. The major looked tired, Frank Garland thought and was not surprised. "The first is this: Senator Mark Hardin will arrive from Washington on this evening's train. His ostensible purpose is to attend his son's wedding. Lieutenant Hardin is now a prisoner of the Sioux—as far as we know."

Major Kingman paused here and allowed his gaze to swing thoughtfully across the faces of the officers in front of him. Gil Hardin had not been popular with his brother

94

officers but, if any of them were either glad or sorry that Gil would not be present at any wedding right now, it did not show in their faces.

He went on.

"Senator Mark Hardin is a powerful and influential man in Washington. In the past he has been accustomed to dictating to the Army when it suited him to do so. Furthermore, there are certain selfish interests at work in the east which would like to see the Indians stirred up to the point where the Army would have to take the field against them again in a full-scale campaign. Senator Hardin is, I am sorry to say, associated with those interests. Until now he and his friends have lacked the necessary excuse to make the move which they contemplate. Lieutenant Hardin's capture has now provided them with that excuse, gentlemen."

A pregnant silence greeted the major's words as the officers shuffled their feet a little and waited for him to go on.

Garland said bluntly, "Senator Hardin is not going to be pleased to hear of what has happened to Gil. What do you expect he'll do, major?"

Major Kingman placed his hands on the desk, palms down, and squared his shoulders.

"There are a great many things that I expect he will do, captain. The thing that I fear most is that he will have this garrison ordered into the field against the Sioux bands still peaceably remaining on the reservation. That would be tragic."

"Can he do that?"

"A man with Senator Hardin's prestige can do almost anything where the Army is concerned, Captain Garland," Major Kingman said, clipping his words a little. "The fact that such an action would defeat its own purpose—would precipitate the calamity which we are trying to avoid—will, I am afraid, mean nothing to the senator."

He paused for a moment, rolling a pencil thoughtfully beneath his finger tips and frowning a little as he again arranged his thoughts in his mind. When he spoke again, his voice was crisp and sure and Frank Garland knew that the major had made up his mind. There would be no going back.

"Our only hope of getting Lieutenant Hardin alive and of preventing the outbreak of a general war is to hit Broken Feather and his band. Scatter them. Bring Feather and his subchiefs in here to Fort Duncan. With winter coming on, the rest will then drift back to the reservation—they will have no other choice. Through good luck, we have learned where the band is now holed up and, if we punish them sufficiently, other bands will be discouraged from leaving the reservation. They are wavering now."

Captain Babson, who commanded L Company, cleared his throat harshly. "Will the whole garrison go out, major?" Major Kingman shook his head.

"A single company will best be able to accomplish this mission," he said decisively. "It will stand the best chance of surprising Broken Feather and surprise is essential if we are to accomplish our purpose. You will agree, gentlemen, that the assignment properly belongs to Company K."

"When do we march, sir?" Garland asked.

"K will be prepared to march early tomorrow," Major Kingman said quietly and let a silence fall over the room for a moment. Then he stood up, clasped his hands behind his back. "You have wondered why I did not start a column immediately to effect Lieutenant Hardin's rescue. I had my reasons. First, the location of Broken Feather's band was not then known. More important, any general expedition by this garrison would be likely to drive the rest of the disaffected bands off the reservation. But there was an overriding reason above all of these!"

Major Kingman looked at each of the officers in front of him in turn. *This is it,* Frank Garland thought. *The Old Man is going to burn his bridges behind him now.*

Major Kingman said slowly, "That reason is this. As long as I remain in command here, not one soldier stirs out of Fort Duncan to rescue Mark Hardin's son until I have the senator's personal promise that this thing which he has planned is dead! That there will be no new land grab now!

That his agents—such as Arco Blaine—will stop furnishing whiskey and guns to the Indians and inciting them to make new medicine for war! I want those promises from him, gentlemen! I mean to have them! Are there any questions?"

Garland and Oglethorpe Henderson walked back across the parade ground together. The major had granted Henderson permission to ride with K when and if the company rode out. Frank Garland was glad of that. Thorpe Henderson was a good man to have along when the chips were down.

Henderson said, "Can he do it, Frank? Get away with facing Senator Hardin down like that?"

"No," Frank Graland said. "He'll be relieved of command as soon as Mark Hardin can get a wire to Washington and back. He knows that. But somebody's got to have the guts to make the try."

"A sad business," Thorpe murmured.

They went on into the orderly room. The barracks were noisy as men came in from drill, the sober events of the morning now forgotten or pushed into the backs of men's minds. Garland called out and, after a minute, First Sergeant Bestwood came in.

"We've got the word, Jim," Garland said with a faintly sardonic good humor. "K will probably move out at daybreak tomorrow. How many men will we muster?"

"Sixty-two," Sergeant Bestwood told him with the lines in his face loosening a little. "Morrison and Fogarity are in the hospital. The Dutchman, Schmidt, is in the guardhouse."

"Since when and for what?" Garland asked sharply.

"Since last evening and for fightin' in town," Bestwood answered in a grim voice. Garland allowed himself a faint smile.

"Get him out, Jim. There'll be no furniture that he can break up where we're going. And we've got too few old hands to ride tomorrow, as it is. How did the recruits do on the range this morning?"

"Bledsoe is still shuttin' his eyes when he squeezes off," Jim Bestwood grunted. "McNamara an' Glotz handle their pieces like they were pushing stable brooms. Sampson couldn't hit a bull in the tail with a fiddle. For recruits they're doin' well."

"They'll do a hell of a lot better after they get back from this ride," Garland told him cheerfully. "Usual loads. A hundred rounds per man for the carbines. Eighteen per pistol. Each man will take twelve pounds of oats. Toronto Peters will ride with us. So will Lieutenant Henderson."

Sergeant Bestwood nodded his head and paused at the door to give Oglethorpe Henderson a faint nod. "I'm glad to hear that, sir," he said heavily. "Like the captain says there'll be all too few old hands riding with K tomorrow."

After Bestwood went out, Garland turned to Oglethorpe Henderson. "You sure that you want to come along on this, Thorpe? It'll be a hell of a hard ride, and you don't look too fit yet."

Henderson waved a careless hand. "I'll make out all right, Frank," he said. "It's kind of a family matter, isn't it? With Gil touching it off the way he did?"

Garland gave him a quick, hard look. "Yes, it's a family matter," he said.

Henderson squinted at the end of his cigarette. "I heard about what happened last night," he said. "Arco tried to beef you, Frank—the way I heard it."

Garland scowled. "O'Garragh talks too much," he grumbled. "Well, whiskey and gunrunning isn't all that Arco Blaine's tied up with, it seems. According to Charley, he's got a string on Gil—figures to use him to bargain with. To whom and for what, I'm damned if I know. Got any ideas, Thorpe?"

"I've got a big one," Henderson said. "Don't you figure that Senator Mark Hardin would pay plenty to get Gil back, Frank? He might even use his influence to get Arco Blaine's commission restored to him. Ever think of that?"

Frank Garland's face darkened with anger. He said softly, "Arco Blaine will never wear the uniform again if I have to kill him first, Thorpe!"

Out in the long room of K's barrack the word had already spread. Trumpeter Monk Walters had flopped down on his bunk, hands behind his head and a cigarette in his mouth. "Glory, here I come," he said to no one in particular. "Why can't they just let us whitewash the rocks around the flagpole and shovel out the stables and do other soldier chores like that? Why do we always have to go out and fight with somebody? Me, I'm a peaceable man. I ain't mad at nobody."

"What's the matter, Monk?" a trooper called from across the aisle as he ran a patch back and forth through the barrel of his carbine; squinted critically at the shining bore. "You mean that you got somebody who'll miss you when you're dead, boy?"

"Don't know what you're talking about," Monk Walters answered airily. "Nobody dies. Me, I'll live forever."

"What's forever?"

"It's a long time," Monk Walters told him. "It's a thousand beers lined up in a row on a bar. It's a year of Sunday afternoons while you walk out with your girl on your arm back home."

Corporal O'Garragh grunted—he and Monk Walters were friends. "Where's back home?" he asked. "I never knew you had a home. I figured they must have found you under a beer keg somewhere."

"Springfield, Massachusetts," Monk Walters said dreamily. "That's where it is. They got trees there—great big green ones—and grass growing out in front of the houses. A pretty, pretty town, Mister O'Garragh."

"You won't see it again," O'Garragh said.

Farther along the line of bunks, Trooper Paul Fraley sat quietly, smoothing the palm of his hand up and down across the sleek stock of his carbine. He was vaguely excited—and a little scared. Now, he was going out to fight. . . . Like Georgie Jarvis had gone.

He ought to tell Annie Helfron about it, he guessed.

Corporal Greenbriar, his face casual, strolled into the sutler's store. As he had expected, Yancy Donovan—an old man who did odd jobs for La Farge, the sutler—was sitting in a corner. Corporal Greenbriar ordered two cigars, paid La Farge's squaw for them, and then went on out, jerking his head at Yancy Donovan as he went. After a moment, Donovan followed.

They talked in the little lean-to which the sutler used as a storeroom behind the store. Corporal Greenbriar rested his back against a pile of kegs while he looked at the old man with eyes which were bright and hard.

"You going back to town today, Yancy?"

"Reckon to." The old man's eyes shifted nervously.

"You might bump into Arco Blaine there?"

Yancy Donovan looked scared. "There was a little trouble last night," he mumbled. "Arco's took to the hills, I guess."

"But you might just run into him, Yancy?"

Corporal Greenbriar's voice was insistent now, his eyes mean. "I guess I might," Yancy said. "A man never knows."

"Tell him that Senator Mark Hardin is coming in on the evening train, Yancy," Corporal Greenbriar said. "Tell him that Whitewater Charley is spilling all he knows in the guardhouse here. Tell him that K marches tomorrow. Have you got all that?"

"Yeah, I got it," Yancy said.

Greenbriar gave him another bright look. "See that you don't forget it." He walked out of the lean-to and started back across the parade ground, whistling softly.

He had no love for Arco Blaine—just as he had no love for anyone else here at Fort Duncan. But a man picked up a dollar wherever he found one lying around. It was the advantage which a college education gave you, he thought cheerfully.

12. Hotel in Hagar

IT WAS getting on toward four in the afternoon when Frank Garland finished with the last of the papers on his desk—pushed them away from him with a sigh of relief. He was a man who hated paper work—little hen tracks to be made and then filed away somewhere.

And all about as useless as a fifth leg on a horse, he thought sourly. Then the memory that K would be riding again tomorrow came back to him and he stretched his arms over his head and allowed the yawn to leave his lips in a grin. Good to be on the trail again with the scouts out ahead and the flankers moving on either side. To hear the jangle of gear behind him and the snort of the horses and the rough banter of the troopers as they rode at ease, dust caked on their faces and their eyes squinted into the sun. A man lived then.

Sergeant Jim Bestwood came in saying, "Hitchcock wants to see you" and Garland nodded and said, "Send him in." He was not surprised. Hitchcock was the Old Man's orderly—probably come with some further word about the march tomorrow.

Hitchcock, a lanky and sad man, stood just inside the doorway and fixed his eyes—liquid, like those of a dog—on Frank. "The major's compliments, sir," he said, "and will the captain report to the major at his quarters at once."

Something in the doleful expression on the man's face warned Frank as he nodded and reached for his hat. He went on across the parade ground, Hitchcock trailing at his heels, and a thread of uneasiness began to run through him as he went. Major Kingman was not a commander who bothered his subordinates with unnecessary conferences on the eve of a march. Something new had come up, something important enough to cause the major to call Frank away from the last-minute chores which the major knew, better than anyone, attended a man's departure into the field with a column.

Major Kingman was at the door as Garland came up; "Come on in, Frank," he said with unusual abruptness, and stalked on ahead into the small room which served him as an office.

"Frank," he said angrily, "take a look at this! By Heaven, it would have been better if that court-martial had ordered the man shot three years ago!"

He tossed the faintly soiled note, which Yancy Donovan had given to Janet Davenport, across the desk and waited while Garland picked it up and read it. When Garland had done, he laid the single sheet of paper back and gave a full attention to the major again.

"Well?" he asked softly.

"Maggie found it on the dresser in Janet's room," Major Kingman exploded. "Of all the colossal conceit, the infernal nerve of that fellow."

Frank Garland stirred his shoulders a little. "It's the sort of thing that I'd expect of Arco Blaine," he murmured, wondering a little why it should upset Major Caleb Kingman so. "He ran into Miss Davenport and myself as we were coming from Hagar yesterday. You told her to pay no attention to it?"

Major Kingman glared at him, then shook his head and took a red handkerchief from his pocket and mopped his face with it. "I have told that young woman nothing," he growled. "She isn't here—she's gone on into Hagar to meet him."

Frank Garland's mouth thinned out into a hard line. "Tell me more about it," he said.

Major Kingman swung a hand violently. "I don't know any more! Hitchcock saw her walking toward the sutler's store a half-hour ago. Then, when Maggie found this confounded note, she sent for me. I went to the sutler's store myself—just got back from there. The sutler's squaw told me that Janet had left for Hagar with Yancy Donovan a few minutes before. Take a squad and ride into town and bring the little fool back, Frank!"

"No good, sir," Garland said abruptly. "A squad would fall over its own feet. I'll ride in alone."

He saw the swift relief which flowed into Major Kingman's face; saw, too, how the Major had aged in the last twenty-four hours. The knowledge angered him suddenly. Damn it, he thought, hasn't he got enough on his shoulders already without this? He swung away to take his departure.

Marjory Kingman met him in the hall to drop a hand on his arm. "Don't make this your fight, Frank," she said, lifting sober eyes to him. "Be careful, won't you?"

Garland's mouth smoothed out flatly and a meanness came into his eyes. "Arco Blaine has always been my fight, Maggie," he said roughly and swung on out of the room.

After he had gone, Marjory Kingman went slowly to the window and looked onto the parade ground, watching Garland's lean form as he went on toward the barracks. When she spoke her voice was low and faintly sad, "Frank is in love with her, Caleb. He doesn't know it yet himself but he is. I could see it in his eyes."

Caleb Kingman stared at his wife for a long moment, his forehead wrinkled a little and his eyes disturbed. Then he said finally, "You're not often wrong about things, Maggie. Should I call him back and send another officer?"

She smiled a little sadly and shook her head. "You couldn't call him back if you wanted to, Caleb," she said.

Frank Garland was scowling as he went across the parade ground with a long, full stride. She must be damned well in love with Gil Hardin, he thought morosely—but then she didn't know Arco Blaine for what the man was. Maybe you couldn't blame her too much. And then the thought of her meeting the man sent a quick sickness into the pit of his stomach and he concentrated instead on things to be done.

Corporal McNair was at the stables, waiting for Stable Call. Garland curtly ordered him to saddle the bay. Then he turned on back to the orderly room. Jim Bestwood was there.

"I'm riding into Hagar," Garland told him curtly. "Mc-Nair will follow with the light wagon."

Bestwood nodded, narrowing his eyes a little as Garland buckled his gun belt about his waist. "Will the captain inspect the men tonight?" he asked.

"At eight," Garland said shortly. "And I'd better not find so much as a button missing, Bestwood! See to it!" He swung about abruptly and was gone.

First Sergeant Jim Bestwood stared after him, rubbing his craggy chin thoughtfully. *By God,* he thought, *something is riding the man with a rough spur. Warning ME there'll be no gear missing on the night before a march!*

Back at the stables, the bay was saddled and Garland gathered the reins and swung on up into the saddle. "Hitch up the light wagon," he snapped over his shoulder to Corporal McNair. "Take it into Hagar and wait by the hotel. Miss Davenport will be coming back with you." He swung his mount around and spurred away.

Janet Davenport sat stiffly erect beside Yancy Donovan in the buckboard clutching the seat for support as the light vehicle jounced over the road toward Hagar. Yancy Donovan, wishing that he could take a chew of tobacco but pretty sure that he hadn't ought to, glanced at her out of the corners of his eyes.

Damn Arco Blaine, he was thinking. Why did he have to do the man's chores? He didn't like this—not a bit. It could get a man into trouble.

Hagar was a scant half mile ahead when Janet spoke for the first time since they had left the sutler's store. "Where will I find Mr. Blaine in Hagar?" she asked in a tight voice, keeping her eyes straight ahead.

The old man shifted uneasily on the seat beside her. "At the hotel, I reckon, miss. Least ways, that's what he told me."

For a moment, panic suddenly gripped Janet as she tried to picture what she could do with a man like Arco Blaine.

She remembered his face as she had first seen it yesterday —remembered the bold, insolent way that his eyes had roved over her and a sudden emptiness bit at the pit of her stomach. She'd been a fool, she thought with gall-like bitterness. Why hadn't she gone to the major? Why hadn't she gone to Frank Garland?

Then a sudden realization struck her. It was because of Frank Garland that she had come! If, somehow, she could lure Arco Blaine to his capture—to his death, even— Frank Garland would be safe! That was why she had come!

The thought warmed her like a drink of raw brandy and, all at once, she felt strong and whole and a woman. *I am a woman now,* she thought. *For the first time in my whole life. Up until now I have been nothing but a child playing with toys.*

And she knew that she loved Frank Garland.

The buckboard was hauling up in front of the hotel now; Yancy Donovan was pulling the team to a stop. A few loungers stared curiously down from the hotel's veranda. The traffic of late afternoon flowed noisily along Hagar's nameless street.

"Please help me down, Mr. Donovan," she said quietly.

Arco Blaine sat in Room 202, leaning arms on the table in front of him while he moodily turned his glass between his fingers. His dark face was sullen—faintly vengeful—as he brooded over the turn that events had taken. He had been a fool to make a play for Frank Garland last night —he had too much at stake to make any missteps now. And last night had been a misstep because that chuckle-headed breed had disappeared. Probably still running, he thought sourly.

His thoughts swung to Janet Davenport, and his mouth twisted dourly. That, too, had probably been a mistake. He had sent that note off by Yancy Donovan on pure impulse, telling himself that she might come and that, through her, he might make some bargain with that old fool out at the post.

But she wouldn't come. He knew that.

105

He'd been crazy to do the thing at all. Old Kingman, instead, would be sending a squad into town to hunt him down. Frank Garland would be riding in to finish the fight that had begun last night. Well, damn him, let him come!

Blaine swore violently and slammed his glass against the wall. It shattered and the drops of whiskey made a four-pointed star against the dingy wall paper. Blaine stared moodily as it slowly spread.

Footsteps came along the corridor outside, then, and their halting cadence told him that Yancy Donovan had returned. He sat back and waited.

The old man entered and stood there uneasily with the door open behind him.

"Well?" Arco said.

"She came all right," Yancy Donovan said.

For a moment, Blaine blinked stupidly, his mind heavy with whiskey. Then he got slowly out of the chair, his lean frame silhouetted against the room's window, and moved around the table to stand in front of Yancy.

"Where is she?" he asked softly.

"Downstairs in the lobby," Yancy told him.

"Why didn't you bring her up here?"

A faintly shocked look spread over Yancy Donovan's seamed face. His eyes slid furtively aside to take in the small room with its tumbled bed; the table with its bottle in the center. The spreading stain which the whiskey had left against the wall. He shook his head.

"I don't reckon she'd come," he said.

Anger flashed across Arco Blaine's face. "If she'll come from Fort Duncan to the lobby, she'll come from the lobby the rest of the way," he said violently. "Go get her!"

Yancy Donovan blinked and fear began to seep into his eyes. His mind groped stupidly for some excuse.

"I had something to tell you first," he quavered. "That feller, Corporal Greenbriar, out to the fort give me a message for you. Said I wasn't to forget it."

"Well, tell it," Blaine said roughly. "And don't take all day in the telling!"

Triumph was running strong in him, now. Janet Davenport had come to him here. His imagination, inflamed by the whiskey, began to run. It was not the first time that he had called and a woman had come to him.

Yancy was saying haltingly, "Greenbriar said to tell you that Whitewater Charley is in the guardhouse at the fort and that K is marchin' out tomorrow after young Hardin an'——"

"Let them march," Blaine said, his mouth tipping up a little. "Go down and bring that girl up here."

"That ain't all, Arco," Yancy said hurriedly, pushing a hand out as though to ward off a blow. "He said particular to tell you that Senator Hardin is comin' on the train to-night."

"What!"

"That's what he told me, Arco. I swear to God, he did."

Arco Blaine turned suddenly and moved back into the room to sit with his hip on a corner of the table—scowling a little as his mind played with this newest bit of information. It was the break that he had been looking for, he was thinking. This changed a lot of things.

It had been sheer impulse which had prompted him to send that note to Janet, a vague striking back against the fate which had made him an outcast here in this land and had forbidden him association with women like her. A faint hope, perhaps, that the fact that he could help Gil might buy that association back for a little while.

But that was changed now. For she had come. And once again he had drawn to a poor hand and won.

For with old Mark Hardin here at hand—and with his son, Gil, a prisoner of the Sioux—he could dictate his own terms. He'd go down to Janet Davenport himself now. He'd charm her as he had charmed a hundred other women—for women were all the same—and he'd send her to the Senator to bargain for him. Gil's life in return for the things that he wanted. . . .

Then the thought of Whitewater Charley, in the guardhouse at Fort Duncan—Charley who could guide a column to where Feather was holed up—crossed his mind and he scowled again. But his ill-humor didn't last—he knew Fort

Duncan as he knew the palm of his own hand and he'd get the breed loose tonight. It wouldn't be hard and then he'd have the chips that he needed.

A rap at the door interrupted his thoughts and he swung impatiently around. "Who is it?" he demanded.

"Janet Davenport," a woman's voice said firmly. "I wish to come in, Mr. Blaine."

Her voice did something to him all at once—it was low and soft as he had known that it would be. He called, "Just a minute, Miss Davenport," and then said under his breath to Yancy Donovan, "When she comes in, you get out—fast! And keep your mouth shut!"

13. A Fight in a Room

ARCO BLAINE went on past the old man to open the door and Janet stood there, her face pale beneath the bonnet as she looked at him. Yancy Donovan scuttled past her like a rabbit and the corridor echoed with the sound of his boot heels as he turned for the stairs, running hard.

I've got to go through with this now, Janet was thinking in the moment that she stood there. *I've gone too far to turn back.*

Her senses were acutely aware of the things around her, an aura which held her. The musty smell of the corridor along which forgotten men—and women—had passed going their ways. The sheen of the fading sunlight on the window across the room where dust made its cobwebby smears against the glass. The table with its bottle; the smell of spilled whiskey which came like a sweetly evil stench to her nostrils. And finally, Arco Blaine standing there in front of her, his lips smiling recklessly beneath the thin line of his mustache and his eyes hotly cataloguing her.

He said, "Will you come in, Miss Davenport?" and, hardly knowing what she did, she nodded and passed by him into the room. Heard him close the door.

"I have to talk to you, Mr. Blaine," she said then as she turned to face him. "That is why I have come."

He smiled at her and she was suddenly aware that there were little sparks which came and went at the backs of his eyes. "Of course," he said. "I had hoped that you would come, Miss Davenport."

He gestured toward the single chair, but Janet shook her head. "I prefer to stand," she told him in a voice which wasn't quite steady. "You had something to tell me about Lieutenant Hardin?"

For a moment Arco considered that, leaning a hand against the window's edge while he looked at her, his gaze sultry and brooding a little. Then he said abruptly, "You are a beautiful woman, Miss Davenport. You know that, of course. Many men have told you."

Janet felt the blood begin to rise in her face and a sort of helpless anger ran through her. Again that cold hand squeezed her stomach and suddenly she wished desperately that she could turn and see Frank Garland standing there in the doorway behind her.

"I did not come here to discuss myself," she said and the words sounded feeble and inane in her own ears. Arco Blaine was smiling lazily at her now.

"It is a subject that I would have liked to pursue," he murmured and she knew hotly that he was laughing at her. "However, I am at your service."

She swung back to him, a glimmer of hope springing up in her as an idea came into her mind. "I have heard of you, Mr. Blaine," she said, spacing her words a little and lifting her chin. "I know that you were court-martialed and dismissed from the Army." She saw the dark blood which flooded into Arco Blaine's face with sudden violence but she hurried on, her words coming faster now. "Senator Hardin, the lieutenant's father, is coming here on the train tonight. If you'll promise to leave Hagar—now, tonight— I'll intercede with him in your behalf. Perhaps he could get you a pardon——"

Her voice faltered then at tempestuous anger which she saw in the man's face as he started toward her. "Madam," he said, his voice shaking, "I don't need you—or anyone else—to beg my pardons for me! I shall demand them for myself! And I'll get them—and in my own way!"

Real terror held her now as she backed away toward the door. For the man who was coming toward her was not the same man who had been lounging there by the window seconds before and with a careless smile on his lips. There was a brand of madness in his eyes.

Frank Garland tied the sweating bay at the hitch rail in

front of the Deerfoot and went in, slamming the doors roughly back. Toronto Peters, the civilian scout, was slouched lazily at the far end of the bar with a bottle and a glass in front of him.

He said, "Howdy, Frank. What's the matter? Rattlesnake bite you?"

Garland brushed that aside. "Have you seen Yancy Donovan?" he demanded roughly.

Toronto Peters looked at him quizzically—he was a man who could not be hurried. Then he answered, "He was in here maybe ten minutes ago, Frank. Looked like he'd just seen a spook. He downed three drinks fast and then went out again like the devil had hold of his coat tail. What you want him for?"

"To kill him!" Frank Garland said between his teeth and swung the weight of his displeasure onto the fat bartender who was methodically mopping his bar rag up and down. "Where does he hang out in town, Finn?"

"Up at Lamarr's livery stable," Finn said imperturbably and went on with his mopping.

Garland whirled and went out.

A hundred yards up the street, the livery stable's door made a dim square against the last of the afternoon's sun, an opening pungent with the ammonia smell of stabled animals as Garland went in. He called roughly, "Donovan! Where are you, Donovan?" and waited a moment for his answer.

None came and he turned abruptly into a small harness room which opened off to one side. Dimmer still in here but his eyes were accustomed to the gloom now and he saw old clothes huddled in one corner and he reached a long arm and hauled Yancy Donovan out.

"Where'd you take Miss Davenport, Yancy?" he demanded in a dangerous voice.

"I don't know nothing, captain!" Yancy quavered. "I swear I don't know nothing! I didn't do nothing——"

Garland slapped him, hard. "Where'd you take her? I swear, I'll break your skinny neck if you don't tell me!"

"To the hotel, captain," Yancy Donovan said in a dull

voice then. "That's where I took her. Arco told me to."

There was something in the old man's voice which told Garland that he was telling the truth and he dropped him like an empty grain sack and turned away. Yancy scuttled back to the safety of the harness room; huddled there, shivering while he listened to the hollow sound of Frank's boot heels dying away on the stable boards.

He'd have to get out of town fast now, Yancy Donovan was thinking miserably. Arco Blaine would be after him and Arco would do a lot more than slap.

The hotel's lobby was deserted except for the clerk behind the desk as Garland went by in long strides; started up the stairs. The clerk's eyes were worried as he watched Frank go past.

There was the hallway, remembered from last night but lighted now by the smudged window at the far end instead of the smoky lamp in its bracket. And midway down the corridor was Room 202 with its door closed on whatever it was that went on inside. For a moment Garland paused with his hand on the knob while he listened.

Then Janet Davenport's voice called urgently, "No! No!" and Garland flung the door back.

Janet's face was white and stiff as she turned slowly toward him. Arco Blaine, stood in the middle of the room silhouetted against the window's light, his face dark with anger. The table and the whiskey bottle and the stale smell of liquor in the room sickened Frank as he looked. He didn't know what he had expected; he had not expected this. Janet here alone in a room with Arco Blaine who boasted of his women.

He dropped his hand to the gun at his hip; drew it and swung its muzzle to cover Arco. "Stand still, Blaine," he said harshly.

Then he was vaguely aware that Janet was saying, "Frank! Frank! I'm so glad that you've come——"

"Corporal McNair is waiting in front of the hotel with the light wagon, Miss Davenport," he heard himself saying through stiff lips. "Will you go down to him, please? He will take you back out to the post."

112

"Yes," Janet said dully. This was a Frank Garland that she had not seen before. She went past him and out into the corridor.

As she went slowly down the stairs and across the small lobby she was acutely aware that the clerk was watching her out of the corner of his eyes. She felt dirty, humiliated, as she passed on out into the late sunlight where Corporal McNair, his craggy face impassive, waited to help her into the wagon.

Ahead of her was the depot, its unpainted boards bleached by too much sun and leaning a little awry, and suddenly she felt a wild impulse to go there and wait on the benches until the train came to take her from this terrible land.

Corporal McNair saluted. "You ready to go back to the post, ma'am?" She nodded dumbly and allowed him to help her across the wheel and into the seat. McNair climbed to the front seat and unwound the reins from the brake.

"Hup, Bess!" he said imperturbably. "Sam!"

A cowboy went by on the rickety sidewalk, his boot heels scraping and his eyes glancing quickly at her and then veering away as he passed. In the Deerfoot, a man laughed with a sudden lifting of sound as they passed, then the wagon rolled on out onto the flat dunness of the prairie.

Oh, heavens, Janet was thinking dully, *Frank believes that I went there to keep an assignation with Arco Blaine. What else can he ever believe?*

Garland closed the door with the back of his heel after Janet had gone; moved forward toward Arco Blaine with his eyes ice-cold now. For a moment neither spoke; then Blaine laughed shortly and lunged forward a little toward the table.

"You have a fondness for interfering in my business, Frank," he said between his teeth. "I am tired of that."

"I'll interfere until I have run you out of this country," Garland told him in a tight voice. "Or have seen you put under six feet of ground."

"No, Frank," Arco Blaine said thinly. "I don't think you will. I hold top cards in this game now. When Senator Hardin steps off that train tonight, you're through. That old fool, Kingman, is through, too. The two of you sent the senator's precious son out to get captured by the Sioux. Do you think that he will forgive that?"

Frank Garland put a hard rein onto his anger as he watched the other man with narrowed eyes.

He could see something that was shadowed at the back of Arco Blaine's eyes—an uncertainty, perhaps a forlorn hope. And, for a moment, Frank Garland was almost sorry for this man who had once ridden beside him but who had now cast himself out of the ranks of honest men. Then Arco Blaine laughed and Garland's mind hardened.

"I'm Mark Hardin's man out here, Frank," Blaine was saying now. "I'm the one who persuaded Feather to jump the reservation. And I'm the only one who can get the senator's son back for him alive. I will do that—for a price!"

"What price?"

"My commission back!" Arco Blaine said violently. "The Army robbed me of that—I will have vindication! That's the price I want from Senator Mark Hardin. From all of you!"

"The bargains that you make with the senator are your own," Garland said in a brittle voice. "You make no bargains with me. I am still waiting for an answer to my question, Arco. I want it. What was Miss Davenport doing with you here in this room?"

For a moment Arco Blaine stared back at him; then shook his head. "You would not believe me if I told you, would you, Frank?"

"I have never believed you," Garland told him harshly. "All I'm waiting for is to hear the lie so I can beat it back between your teeth." He added brutally, "Betraying your trust where women are concerned comes easy to you, doesn't it, Arco?"

He saw the slow red which crawled up into the other's face and he knew that Blaine was remembering—thinking

114

back to that night at Fort Corse. Then Blaine flung out a hand in a violent gesture.

"You talk big with a gun in your hand, Frank."

Garland grunted; holstered the gun and unbuckled his belt with slow fingers. The holstered gun dropped to the floor and he kicked it into a corner and lunged hard across the room.

His swinging fist sledged at Blaine's face but the man dodged away and Frank felt the hot pain as Blaine's knuckles slammed into the side of his neck. Then a slugging left hand found its mark in Blaine's belly and the man grunted and staggered back against the wall.

Garland beat him with jolting blows to the head and grunted a little as he felt the shock run through knuckles and wrists. Blood marked Arco Blaine's mouth now but, through it, his white teeth snarled and Garland smashed at them wickedly.

The table went over with a crash and, from a far distance, Frank could hear the sound of men's yelling and the shuffle of feet on the stairs. He said hoarsely, "Come on and fight Arco! You're not dealing with women now!"

Arco fell back from a right hand blow that drove him half-across the room; then seized the chair and swung it over his head. Garland ducked and took the blow on his left forearm and felt his shoulder go numb as the chair splintered.

There was a salty taste of blood in his mouth now as he felt two of Arco Blaine's blows rack home past his useless left hand. It didn't matter. Blaine's face was square in front of him now and he drove his right hand full at it and felt the jolt move up into his shoulder. Blaine went down to his knees, shaking his head slowly back and forth while he retched in great sobs.

"Get up, Arco!" Garland said hoarsely, a violent urgency in his voice now. "Get up and fight, damn you!"

Blaine's voice was coming to him then across a great distance. "I'm through, Frank," he said.

For a moment Frank Garland stood there, looking down at him. "I'm sorry that I could not kill you," he said. "I'll take you on back to the post instead where you'll probably hang. It is what you deserve."

He turned and started toward where his gun lay in the corner as voices boiled up in the corridor outside. And he knew, then, that he had made a mistake. From the corner of his eye he caught, too late, a glimpse of the thrown bottle. It exploded against his temple and he sagged to his knees with weakness running like water through him as the door slammed back and men boiled into the room. Then Arco Blaine was crowding his way through the press and was gone, the sound of his boot heels echoing back above the noise of the room.

A man stood over him, saying, "You all right, captain?" He nodded without speaking and got back to his feet, swaying a little, and then sat on the edge of the bed while he waited for the racketing to go out of his head.

Toronto Peters shouldered his way into the room, carrying a bottle by the neck, and said, "You look like hell, Frank. What happened? Here, have a shot of this."

"Get these people out of here, Pete," Garland told him tiredly.

They went reluctantly, the thin clerk complaining in a high and angry voice, "Somebody's got to pay for this mess!" Garland lifted a hand toward him.

"Send the bill to Arco Blaine," he said through puffed lips and the man finally went.

When they were all gone Toronto Peters closed the door. The whiskey bit deep at Frank—he shook his head and drank again and placed the bottle on the floor. Finally he stood up and buckled the gun belt about his waist. Toronto Peters squinted at him from beside the window.

"You look like hell, Frank," he said again. "I got to say that Arco looked worse, though. He went by me down below like a spook was chasin' him. What happened?"

Garland lifted a hand to feel of his face and then grinned wryly. "We had a little argument, Pete," he answered. "Where was Arco headed the last you saw of him?"

Toronto spat on the littered floor. "Headed for parts un-

116

known, I guess you might say," he grunted. "You sure worked him over good, Frank."

Garland shook his head and scowled. "I lost my head," he admitted sourly. "I should have kept a gun on him and hauled him on out to the post. Now, somebody will have to run him down all over again, Pete."

"I wouldn't bet that they'd find him," Toronto Peters grunted. "The way he was goin' when I seen him last he ought to be out of Dakota Territory by now."

Garland picked up his hat and clapped it onto his head, wincing a little. For a moment he stood, the whiskey pushing strength back into his knees, while he looked at the room's wreckage. Then he turned abruptly away.

"He won't go far, Pete," he said in an absent voice. "He's got too much of a stake around here now—I found that out the hard way. Let's get out of here."

They went on down the stairs, crossed the deserted lobby and went on out onto the hotel's veranda. Far out on the prairie a locomotive's whistle sounded and, to the east, the plume of sooty black smoke was flattening itself out in the wind.

"Hear that Gil's paw is comin' on that," Toronto Peters said drily. "Maybe he'd like to ride along with K tomorrow an' lead a charge like Gil did, Frank."

"Maybe he would," Garland answered absently.

The clatter of shod horses was coming into town now and, after a moment, the fours of a column of cavalry entered Hagar's nameless street, the troop horses dancing a little and the troopers sitting straight and stiff beneath their dress helmets. It was M, coming in as an escort to the senator, Garland thought tiredly. Walt Whittaker, commanding M, lifted a hand as he rode by the two men standing on the hotel's veranda and Frank could see the curiosity in the other officer's eyes.

Then the tail of the column was past and the street was specked with latecomers hurrying toward the train's arrival. Garland shrugged. Another day, he thought sourly. A man had only so many of them.

"Come on, Pete," he said.

14. In the Army Nobody Dies

RETREAT had already gone when Garland and Toronto
Peters reached the main gate. Frank allowed the scout to
take his horse on to the stables while he went on slowly
across the empty parade ground on foot. From the barracks
came the cheerful racket of men at their evening meal. The
clatter of mess gear and the rise and fall of voices, robust
and profane, and all of the other sounds that three hun-
dred-odd men make when the day's work is over and the
evening's play lies ahead.

The wind was colder—more biting against his face now,
Frank thought absently. And there was something new in
it. A veiled warning which was more than just the harsh
promise of coming winter; a whisper that said that a blizzard might be on its way. The sun, going down behind the
bare flagpole, had a red eye to it tonight; for a last moment
it hung in a scarlet orb before it took its final plunge behind
Coyote Butte off to the west.

They would ride that way tomorrow.

Garland went on, meeting no one and glad of that; he
had no wish at this moment to stop for explanations. His
battered face smarted painfully beneath the nip of the wind
now. Smoke was coming from the chimney of Major Kingman's quarters, a gray plume which the wind snatched
away and flattened angrily.

He kicked open the door of his own quarters and stood
for a moment just inside the doorway, feeling again that
dislike for the bare cheerlessness of the place. Then he
closed the door behind him. He mixed whiskey and stale
water from the bucket and sat for a moment with his drink
in the rawhide chair while he scowled soberly at the bare

118

wall opposite and allowed his mind to go back over the events of the last hour.

His thoughts went in circles but the circles always turned on themselves to come back to Janet Davenport. He could see her as she had stood there in that room of the hotel in Hagar and each time he pushed his thoughts on past that point with a little pang. He knew why she had gone there —but that did not ease the fact that she had been there. In that room alone with Arco Blaine.

Damn the man! He dirtied everything that he touched. Quick rage ran through Garland like a hot flash and for a moment again he passionately wished that he had killed Arco Blaine in that room back there. Then his anger passed once more leaving nothing but gray ashes behind.

He thought: *I have no right to care what she does. She belongs to Gil Hardin. She does not belong to me.*

He finished his drink and stripped off his shirt. In the lean-to washroom, he splashed water over his naked shoulders and chest, toweling himself with impatient vigor. His left forearm carried a livid bruise where the chair had struck him and the mirror showed him that he bore the marks of Arco Blaine's fists on his face.

It didn't matter, he thought sourly. Arco Blaine's face would look worse. Well, there was still work to be done tonight. He pulled on a fresh shirt, buttoning it with impatient fingers; then belted the gun about his waist once more and went out into the coming evening.

The red sun was gone now, leaving a redder sky behind it in the west. Dark clouds were beginning to pile up in the north, he noted, and wondered if it would storm tonight. Well, that didn't matter, either. If the word came, K would ride tomorrow storm or no storm.

He went on across the parade ground and into the orderly room and sat down behind the table which was his desk. Private Fraley, at Sergeant Bestwood's word, brought him a plate of beans from the kitchen and he ate at the desk while he signed the last of the reports which Bestwood had placed for him there. The first sergeant had glanced inscrutably at the lump on Frank Garland's temple, the abrasions on his face, and had kept his counsels to himself. He was a man who knew his business.

Young Fraley came after a while to take the plate back to the kitchen. At the door of the orderly room he paused and asked hesitantly, "Could I speak to the captain a minute, sir?" Garland laid down his pen and sat back to look at the boy in front of him.

"What is it, son?" he asked, his voice faintly kind.

He had noticed young Fraley before. A good kid who would make a good soldier someday. Now a little scared and not quite sure of himself. But he'd learn.

Young Fraley fumbled at the pocket of his blue shirt for a moment; found a frayed and soiled slip of paper there and came back to lay it on the table in front of him. Garland picked it up—saw that it read: "Care of Mrs. Julia Fraley, Oleanthe, Missouri,"—and laid it down again.

"I didn't give the right address when I enlisted at Jefferson Barracks, sir," Fraley said, his words tumbling out now. "I just wanted to get away from Oleanthe, I guess. I thought that maybe I'd better tell the captain so that if—well, Private Jarvis didn't give the right address, either, sir."

Frank Garland nodded gravely. "I see," he said. "I'll take care of it, Fraley."

The young trooper saluted awkwardly, clinging to the empty bean plate in his left hand, and said, "Thank you, sir. I'd—well, I guess I'd feel better," and turned toward the door again but Garland's voice halted him.

"Not worried, are you, trooper?"

Young Fraley turned gray, boy's eyes on him and Frank Garland could see the shadows in their depths. "No, sir," young Fraley answered soberly. "I'm not really worried, sir. Only, I guess that it's just that a man never knows, does he, sir?"

Frank Garland smiled a little at that—a smile faintly sad. "No, trooper. A man never knows. Just remember this, though. A lot of men have ridden out through the main gate at Fort Duncan—and have come riding back in again."

Young Fraley was gone then, the tightness eased a little in his face, but Garland still lounged back in his chair, turning the pen between his fingers and staring through the low window at the dusk which was beginning to seep over the parade ground as the day died into night.

A long day. A longer day tomorrow.

His thoughts followed Fraley. One glimpse behind the curtain, he was thinking. One look at what lay along the back trail of one of those sixty-two men who would ride out with him tomorrow morning. A boy whose mother waited for him back in Oleanthe, Missouri; waited patiently, for what she didn't know. Presently he sighed a little and went back to his reports.

Out in the barrack room, First Sergeant Jim Bestwood had assembled Company K. Now, he stood with his big hands on his hips and his craggy brows shadowing his eyes as he looked at them, laying his stare—old and wise in the ways of soldiers—over the men who were grouped among the bunks.

He said then, his voice heavy and dour, "The captain will make a showdown inspection in here at eight o'clock. Each man will stand by his bunk with his gear laid out, includin' his ammunition. Everything had better be there —an' serviceable."

The lamps, which hung from the barracks rafters, had already been lighted although it was not yet full dark, and the light spilled down palely over the faces of the men who stood in front of First Sergeant Bestwood. The faces of sixty-two men, each an individual and each busy with his own thoughts now.

Little concern in the faces of the old-timers. Corporal O'Garragh, Trumpeter Monk Walters, Brecheen. Faint worry in the faces of those who had never before ridden out against the Sioux. Trooper Bledsoe, there, who was still shutting his eyes when he squeezed his carbine off; Sampson, who couldn't hit a bull in the tail with a fiddle; Mike Hanlon, who read his Bible when he thought that none of the rest were looking.

121

And off at one side sat Trooper Otto Fleigheimer, his heavy face flushed and sullen. Trooper Fleigheimer, whose hitch would be up next month and who had it in mind to go to St. Louis—or maybe even New York—on a spree and who didn't want to ride out with the column tomorrow.

Men, each with his own small thoughts and his own small troubles; his own fears and doubts and ambitions and secrets. Sixty-two of them. They were Company K.

First Sergeant Jim Bestwood was going on in his gravelly voice. "The supply sergeant will replace equipment for any man who has got such that is unserviceable," he said heavily. And then he added, "An' God help the man that the captain catches short of anything when he comes to inspect, for the captain will not!"

The tension eased a little at that and men shifted their feet and a whisper ran here and there among the older hands. Then Bestwood put a palm up for a final word and the rustling quieted again beneath the lamps.

"One thing more. No man will leave the barrack here until after the captain is finished. Is that clear?"

Monk Walters asked then, the lamp light glinting on his yellow hair and bright eyes, "And how about afterwards, sarge? Do I get a pass to go down and say good-by to all the girls in Hagar? I wouldn't want to break their hearts."

Laughter ran through the gathered men and First Sergeant Bestwood's craggy face relaxed a little. "You do not, Trumpeter Walters," he said with mock severity. "You will be in your bunk where you belong this night," and he wheeled and went on back to the orderly room. A man like Trumpeter Monk Walters was a priceless thing in an outfit which was a little edgy on the eve of a fight, he was thinking. A little laughter now and then could be better than whiskey.

Back by his bunk, Otto Fleigheimer sat scuffing the toe of his boot into the hard earth while he scowled vacantly at nothing. He was a heavy man—an indifferent soldier who was often in trouble and who, more than once, had felt the displeasure of Corporal O'Garragh in whose squad he rode. Thirty-eight and hating the Army and hating his

122

officers and hating the thought that he must ride tomorrow when release was so close at hand. Monk Walters, rubbing a polishing rag along the sleek length of his trumpet, came swaggering down the aisle between the bunks, hurling cheerful insults to the men on either side as he came.

Monk Walters was popular in K.

Now, he dropped down on the bunk opposite Otto Fleigheimer and squinted at the other, across the way. "Who's dead, pal?" he asked unconcernedly. "You look like you were at a wake."

Fleigheimer glowered at him. "What business is it of yours?" he demanded in a truculent voice.

"Everybody's business is mine, boy," Walters answered airily, scrubbing away at the trumpet in his hand. "Ain't you heard? They're goin' to make me chaplain of this outfit so that everybody can have a shoulder to cry on. You can start crying any time now that you want to."

A dull flush began to creep up into Fleigheimer's heavy face and he half got up from his bunk but Corporal O'Garragh came along then and he dropped sullenly back. O'Garragh gave him a strict attention for a moment—it paid to keep an eye on Fleigheimer at a time like this, O'Garragh had found.

"What goes on?" he demanded roughly.

Monk Walters grinned and admired the sheen of his trumpet in the yellow lamplight. "The Dutch boy don't want to ride with us tomorrow, I do believe, Mister O'Garragh."

The heavy red stayed in Fleigheimer's face. "Why should I have to ride?" he demanded angrily. "My hitch is up next month! I don't want to get killed just when I'm getting out of this damned outfit! I'm not that crazy!"

A strained silence fell between the three of them for a moment, for men about to ride do not ordinarily talk of such things. Glances passed between O'Garragh and Monk Walters; then Walters said, his voice careless, "Hell, Dutch boy, nobody ever gets killed in the Army. Didn't you know that?"

"I will this time," Fleigheimer said despondently, his

123

beefy face drawn into heavy lines. "I can feel it in my bones. I'm going to get it just the same way that Benson and Jarvis got it. A man can tell about such things."

Corporal O'Garragh grunted, "The spooks have got you, is all. What you need is a good dose of salts."

"I don't need any dose of salts," Fleigheimer retorted angrily. "Didn't you see that red sunset tonight? You know very well that a red sunset's the worst kind of bad luck on the night before a column starts to march!"

Monk Walters moistened the mouthpiece of his trumpet with his tongue, blew a half-dozen soft notes and then took the trumpet down again. "Red sunset. Pink sunset. Blue sunset. They're all the same to me. How about you an' me running out to town after taps tonight, Mister O'Garragh? I'll introduce you into high society."

Corporal Tim O'Garragh grinned sardonically; swung a big fist against Monk's shoulder in a light gesture. "You stay away from town tonight, sonny boy," he said with affection faintly shadowed at the back of his voice—he was fond of Monk Walters. "This outfit is liable to ride out tomorrow without nobody to toot its horn, if you don't."

"You are a hard man, Mister O'Garragh," Monk Walters said mournfully.

He got to his feet and he and O'Garragh wandered down the double line of bunks where men were laying equipment out beneath the lamp light. It was full dark outside now; across the parade ground, the lights had come on in the windows of Officers' Row. The wind still blew.

For five minutes longer, Fleigheimer sat on his bunk, his shoulders hunched and his eyes fixed on the dirt floor. That certainty that he was going to be killed was growing stronger in him now, once he had brought his fear full into the open.

Damn it, the Army had no right to send him out to be killed! Not when his hitch was so nearly up, it didn't! Then an idea crept into his mind insidiously. He wouldn't go! They didn't have any right to make him go! He'd wait until lights were out. Then he'd slip out and run the sentries and get away. They couldn't do this to Otto Fleigheimer!

First Sergeant Jim Bestwood came back to the orderly room after giving his instructions, and Frank Garland signed the last of the reports and pushed them away from him and looked at his watch. Seven o'clock. An hour to go until time for the showdown inspection. He'd wait here, he decided.

He called, "Sergeant Bestwood!" The first sergeant came on in from his own cubbyhole and Garland waved him to the stool which was the room's only other seat. "How're the men feeling tonight?"

"Like always, I guess, sir," Bestwood said and then Garland waved a hand and said, "Smoke, if you want to, Jim. We've got a little time to kill. This could turn out to be a nasty ride tomorrow. Feather isn't going to give up young Hardin without a fight."

"You think that the lieutenant's still alive, sir?" Bestwood asked cautiously.

Garland considered that. "I think so," he said finally. "I know Feather. He's a cagey old devil and he's going to leave himself an out. He left the reservation thinking the other bands would follow. The Uncpapas have but they're small now and not worth much. There's been no general exodus and Feather knows it."

Sergeant Jim Bestwood nodded as he stuffed rank tobacco into his pipe and got the thing going. "None that I've heard of," he agreed heavily.

"Blaine was the one who persuaded Feather to make the break but I've got a hunch that the chief doesn't trust Arco Blaine very much any more. Capturing Lieutenant Hardin was a break for him. If he has to, he'll try to trade the lieutenant off for a safe return to the reservation, I think."

Sergeant Bestwood asked thoughtfully, "Our mission tomorrow is to give him a chance to make that trade?"

Garland shook his head soberly, slouching a little in his chair so that the yellow light fell across the lean, brown planes of his face. "I wish it was that simple, Jim. It's not. We've got to hit Feather and hit him hard. Scatter his band and bring him back in irons. It's too bad but that's the way that it's got to be. If Feather and his people aren't punished now—punished severely—you know what will happen."

Rank blue smoke wreathed First Sergeant Bestwood's grizzled head as he nodded. "Yes, I know," he answered.

Garland went on, speaking half to himself. "This whole situation out here is as touchy as a powder keg, Jim. Feather left the reservation, killed two soldiers, captured an officer. If we let that go unpunished the other bands will take it as a sign of weakness on our part. It won't be a month before the reports will start to trickle in. A stage station burned here. A family scalped there. Finally the whole thing will blow up again."

Sergeant Bestwood nodded again and sighed a little. "It's a hard thing, captain," he said finally. "But one that must be done, I guess. Well, pretty soon the time will come for me to go back to the farm in Iowa and watch while somebody else does the job. And don't think I'll be sorry."

Garland didn't answer that and, for a space, the two sat without talking. The draft, from a freshening gust of wind, sucked through the door to make the flame of the lamp smoke and dance; the sounds of the barrack were a muted murmur behind.

Then Garland said slowly, "You won't go back, Jim. Not as long as you've got teeth enough left to chew your beans and strength enough left to throw a leg over a saddle. For that is the mark that was put upon you when you took the blue and you cannot get away from it. It is a mark upon us all."

Jim Bestwood took the pipe from his lips and ran a hand across his craggy jaw. "Yes," he admitted finally, "that is true. And why is that, sir? For the beans are no good and the pay is not large and a man finds few comforts in the saddle or in garrison, either. Have you ever found an answer for that?"

Garland shook his head regretfully. "There have been

times when I thought that I had, Jim," he murmured. "And then, just when I think that my fingers have touched it, it will slip away beyond my reach again. I think that it is just something that runs in us and that cannot be explained at all. And perhaps we're better off not to look for explanations."

"I think it's a pride, mostly," Bestwood said then in a reflective voice. "Although that makes little sense—— well, I'd better see how the company is getting on, sir."

He got up, the lamp light shining on his gray hair again, and went on through the door. Garland sat still, his head sunk a little towards his chest after the sergeant had gone.

Pride? It could be that, he thought. Pride of membership in this scanty band of forgotten men. Yes, it could be that.

He shrugged the thought away as he lounged to his feet finally and reached for his hat. Almost time now to make the showdown inspection. And God help the trooper found wanting!

15. Senator Mark Hardin

TROOPER HITCHCOCK, Major Kingman's orderly, was waiting in the orderly room for Garland when he and Sergeant Bestwood returned from making the inspection. The soldier, looking more mournful than ever, saluted in the lamplight. "The major's compliments, sir," he said, "and will the captain please report to the major at his quarters at once, sir."

Garland nodded curtly. "Reveille at four tomorrow morning, Jim, unless I send you other word. I'll see you then." He went on out into the night with Hitchcock following him.

A haze had settled over the ground. A score of misty little haloes surrounded the lights across the way and reddened the myriads of stars which hung low above the parade ground. The temperature had dropped another few degrees; Garland decided that they would ride with overcoats tomorrow. He toyed with the idea of going by his quarters to leave his gun and belt; decided that the urgency of the major's message was too great and went on up the hard-packed path with Hitchcock trailing along a pace behind like a faithful dog.

Major Kingman, his face angry and showing signs of strain, met him at the door. "Come in, Frank," he said shortly, and led the way into the front room. A man stood there warming his backside in front of the fireplace, feet spraddled and hands behind him, and Garland knew that this was Senator Mark Hardin.

An older and more ruthless Gil, he decided. But not the soft, fat Washington politician that he had expected. This man looked as tough and hard as Jim Bestwood did. Wideshouldered and tanned and with knobby, hardfisted hands

128

at the ends of thick wrists. No, not pudgy and soft; a rough and violent customer, Garland concluded.

Major Kingman was saying in an expressionless voice, "Senator Hardin, may I present Captain Frank Garland. He is the senior of my officers and will lead the expedition which will go after your son—when I give the word."

Garland did not miss that final phrase. Neither did Mark Hardin, Frank knew for he saw the swift tightening of the big man's lips. Senator Hardin apparently meant to let that issue lie for a moment, however, for he made no mention of it as he swung his leonine head around to fix his flat stare on Frank, making no move to shake hands.

"I have heard of the captain," he said and his tone told Garland that Gil's complaints had not been addressed to Janet alone. Mark Hardin had swung back to the major now. "Kingman, only criminal negligence on somebody's part allowed my son to go out with so small a force that the Sioux were able to take him! He was a capable and efficient officer and an insufficiency of force can be the only answer for his capture! I want to know who was responsible for that. Is this the officer?"

Garland saw the red crawl up into the major's face under the blunt accusation; felt his own anger begin to run. Major Kingman started to reply but Garland moved closer to the senator, making a sharp gesture for the major to wait.

"I gave the orders for the scout that Lieutenant Hardin made," he said evenly. "I personally gave him his detailed instructions. If there is any blame that attaches to that, it belongs to me, senator."

He watched Mark Hardin's heavy stare swing back to him; saw and understood the unbridled rancor in the older man's eyes as he recognized the challenge in the words and accepted it. He remembered other things, too. Arco Blaine working out here for this man—selling whiskey and guns to the Indians. Arco Blaine's taunt: "I'm Mark Hardin's man out here." Remembered Troopers Benson and Jarvis roped across their saddles and his own eyes grew bleak as he faced Mark Hardin across the width of the room.

Major Kingman, his face tired and his eyes old, moved forward to intervene but Garland shook his head at him. "I think that this is between the senator and me, major," he murmured. "If you don't mind, sir."

Maybe this was insubordination of a sort—he had no right to jump in here like this—but he was damned if he was going to let Mark Hardin take the whole of his spite out on Caleb Kingman. The major could court-martial him later, if he wanted to. Right now the play was his.

Mark Hardin seemed to sense that, too, for he turned to face Frank, his feet spread and firmly planted and his jaw outthrust. A fighter, Garland thought grimly. A dirty fighter who kicked and gouged and butted in the clinches. Well, he could fight like that, too!

"I have heard of you, captain," Hardin said, addressing Garland directly for the first time. "What I have heard has not been favorable. It has been damned disgraceful, as a matter of fact. I am not now surprised to find you not only disrespectful but downright insubordinate. I will pass over that for the moment. Will you now explain to me why you sent my son out on a scout so badly prepared that his command was overrun and he was captured?"

"I will tell you why Lieutenant Hardin was captured, senator," Garland said evenly. "It was because he disobeyed orders—worse than that, he violated even the most elementary principles of tactical troop-leading by attacking a force, known to be hostile, without making any attempt first to reconnoiter its position and determine its strength. Had your son returned safely from the scout up the Blackbird, I would have recommended his court-martial. Does that answer your question, Senator Hardin?"

The dark blood surged up into Mark Hardin's face and he moved forward from the fireplace to shove his big fists down onto the table top.

"That is a lie, sir!" he said in a voice which was half strangled. "My son is a good officer!"

"No, it is not a lie," Frank Garland told him, whipping his words with the violence of a lash now. "I buried two men of my company this morning. In all probability, they

130

would be alive at this moment had any other officer been leading that scout up the Blackbird. But the greater guilt lies at your door, Senator Hardin, for you—through Arco Blaine—are the one who is responsible that Broken Feather is off the reservation. Can you deny that? I have Arco Blaine's boast that that is so. And Arco Blaine was telling the truth!"

He saw, by the opaque curtain which had slipped down over Mark Hardin's eyes, that the shot had gone home and for a moment an uneasy silence hung over the room. Garland waited, his face granite hard now, for the senator to speak again. His mind was curiously alert, picking out the small things around him. The sound of a door opening softly somewhere; the way that Marjory Kingman's window curtains hung lifeless in the heat from the fireplace.

Then Mark Hardin said, his voice grating, "That is another lie. Who is Arco Blaine?"

"Your agent out here," Garland told him, biting a little at the words, and again that opaqueness descended over Mark Hardin's eyes. "The man who has been selling whiskey and guns to the Indians, senator. The man who induced Broken Feather to jump the reservation. Do you remember him now?"

"I know of no Arco Blaine," Mark Hardin snapped. "I never heard the name before in my life!"

Garland said softly, "You know him better as Arthur Blanding, senator. He carries your written commission, I believe. Does that name mean anything to you?"

For a moment Mark Hardin stood there, glaring back at Garland. Then he swung violently to Caleb Kingman. "Put this officer in arrest at once, major!" he said hoarsely. "I want him stripped of his rank and insignia immediately and confined in your guardhouse until I have had time to communicate with the Department in Washington! Do I make myself clear?"

Major Kingman moved forward slowly until he was facing Mark Hardin and again Frank Garland noticed how he had aged in the past twenty-four hours. His head was

131

thrown back, though, and Garland saw the flame in his eyes.

The Old Man was a soldier still. A tough soldier!

"No," Major Kingman was saying in a flat voice. "I will not do that, senator. Captain Garland is the most experienced and the best officer in my command. I think that we may as well settle this whole thing now. What Captain Garland has said is true—both about the conduct and actions of your son on the Blackbird expedition and about the activities of Arco Blaine—or Arthur Blanding, if you wish to call him that." Major Kingman paused for a moment. Then his eyes flashed bluely as he added, "And, I think, about your own part in this whole sad business, as well."

The major's voice carried a lash in it now and Garland, watching as he stood a little to one side, saw that it had stopped Mark Hardin for the moment. It was probable, he thought absently, that this powerful, arrogant man had not been spoken to in this fashion in thirty years. Perhaps it had never happened to him before. But the major would lose, Frank Garland knew with anger cutting at him. This was a game in which he couldn't win.

Mark Hardin gestured angrily with a big hand, sputtering a little as he tried to get the words out. "That will be enough of that, major——"

Major Caleb Kingman beat the words down coldly and without lifting his own voice. "Your plan for a land grab has been known to me for some time now, senator. Your plan for an Indian uprising to force the troops into the field has also been known. It is a thing so evil that I would not have believed it had my sources of information not been above question. As a result of these schemes of yours, your son is now a prisoner of the Sioux. I think that we can get him back. I hope that may be so."

Mark Hardin started to speak again but Major Kingman silenced him with a gesture. In the fireplace a log crackled and fell, sending a shower of sparks up the chimney. A clock ticked loudly at the back of the room.

Major Kingman went on.

132

"But I want to say this to you, sir. I have sent no expedition to rescue your son. And, as long as I am in command of this post, not one soldier will stir toward the rescue of Lieutenant Gilbert Hardin until I have your assurance that the land grab will be stopped! That your agents will cease to incite the Sioux to new war! That the circumstances which are responsible for your son's capture and for the death of two men of my command, will not occur again! Is that clear?"

Garland saw the blood pounding in the veins of Mark Hardin's thick neck as the man lowered his head to stare across the table at Caleb Kingman.

"Do you mean to stand there and tell me, Major Kingman," he demanded thickly, "that every member of this garrison is not already out searching for my son?"

"I mean to tell you that no expedition has started to the rescue of Lieutenant Hardin," Major Kingman said again, dropping his words evenly into the lamplight between them. "I mean to tell you that none will start until you have given me the assurance that I have just asked you for. Will you give that to me, sir?"

"By God!" Mark Hardin said hoarsely, looking at Major Kingman as though he was seeing him for the first time. "Well, by God! You petty little satraps get out here in command of some two-bit post and you begin to think that you are God! Gil was right when he wrote me that! Major, I order you to start all available troops after this Indian band immediately! Now!"

"Do I have your promise that this land grab will be stopped, senator?"

"You have my promise for nothing!" Mark Hardin said, his voice coldly controlled now. "Are you going to start the troops moving, major?"

"I am not—until I have your promise."

Senator Mark Hardin's face suddenly flushed with uncontrolled anger. "We'll see about that! I'm wiring the Department in Washington immediately requesting that you be relieved of command of this post. Believe me, major, that request will not be refused. I'm taking it upon myself

133

now to direct that you turn this command over to the next senior officer at once—we'll see whether or not these troops move out after Gil!"

Frank Garland said thinly then, "I am the next senior officer here, senator. My orders would be exactly the same as those of Major Kingman—were I to take command. Which I will not."

Mark Hardin turned his head to lay his glance venomously on Frank again for a long moment. "I consider you to be in arrest, captain," he said coldly then. "Who is the officer next senior to this man, major?"

"Captain Whittaker," Major Kingman said in a tired voice and Garland's heart sank as the import of that struck him. Walt Whittaker was an ambitious man. He would accept the command; he would carry out Senator Mark Hardin's orders. There could be no doubt about that.

Well, that was that, he thought morosely. For himself, he didn't care; but it was the end of the trail for Major Caleb Kingman—and the old man deserved better than this. Better than to be relieved in disgrace by a fool who didn't know what he was doing. By a civilian, at that, who had no authority other than the arrogant power which politics had given him.

Well, it was the major's reward for the years of soldiering under blasting sun; of riding in freezing rain. It was his recompense for the earned promotions which had never come and for the old wounds which would trouble him badly tonight.

Garland said nothing. There was nothing more to say.

Then Janet Davenport's voice suddenly startled him and he turned a little and saw that she had come quietly into the room, Marjory Kingman with her. She paused just inside the doorway so that the lamplight fell on her face and made a bright sheen across her hair. She was looking full at Senator Mark Hardin and her eyes were blazing.

"You do not dare do these things, Senator Hardin!" she said. Her voice was low but it carried with a bell-like clearness and Frank Garland, watching her, felt that same urge

134

of pride run through him which he had felt earlier for Major Kingman.

Mark Hardin swung his heavy head toward her, surprise widening his eyes as he looked. Then annoyance crossed his face and he made a sharp gesture with one of his hands—as though he was brushing aside a troublesome insect—and his voice was curt and impatient as he replied.

"This is none of your business, Janet," he snapped angrily. "I will appreciate it if both of you ladies will leave us alone until we have finished. It is nothing that concerns you."

"It concerns me very much indeed, Senator Hardin," Marjory Kingman said then and crossed the room with a firm, proud step to take her place beside her husband. "I will stay."

Mark Hardin looked at her coldly. "Then do not blame me if you get hurt, madam," he said in a harsh voice. "You may as well know. I have just removed Major Kingman from command of this post for obvious reasons."

"Very obvious indeed, senator," Marjory Kingman said, her head high and her voice even. "So that your rapacity and your greed might run without hindrance."

A dark stain of red crawled slowly up into Mark Hardin's face at her words. "Be quiet, madam," he said roughly. "You don't know what you're talking about."

"Yes, I know what I'm talking about, Senator Hardin," Marjory Kingman said then, speaking with a softness which nevertheless carried through the room with the clearness of a trumpet. "I'm talking about all of the people out here on the frontier—people like Caleb Kingman and Frank Garland and Sergeant Bestwood and Troopers Benson and Jarvis—who were buried this morning—and yes, even about your son, Lieutenant Gilbert Hardin, who made mistakes but who was one of us out here just the same. I'm talking about all of the people who suffer the indignities of this cruel land in order that this country may grow and prosper and become great. I'm talking about all of the little people who lay their lives on the balance for

135

the ideals which you have forgotten or never knew, Senator Mark Hardin. . . .

"I'm talking about the women down on Suds Row who have followed their men out here so that they might have a home to come back to after their riding and their fighting is done. I'm talking about those men in the barracks across the parade ground who eat their wormy beans and their musty bacon and draw their parsimonious pay each month so that people like you, Senator Mark Hardin, can live in comfort and ease in Washington. Oh, yes, I think that I know what I'm talking about.

"And, when you go to bed tonight, I hope that perhaps you will remember these things and will remember that it is you—and the people like you—who tear down the things that we labor for out here. It is you who dig the graves out there in our poor little cemetery. It is you who disgrace the flag that we keep flying out there on its pole. Oh yes, senator, I know what I'm talking about."

Marjory Kingman's voice fell away and, for a moment, a silence settled over the lamplit room. Then Caleb Kingman reached out and touched his wife's arm with a gentle hand.

"It's all right, Maggie," he said and Frank Garland marveled a little at the steady sureness in the major's voice. "We've made a good fight. No one can do more."

Mark Hardin turned angrily to Janet. "Janet, do you realize that these fools have done nothing?" he demanded. "Nothing at all toward effecting Gilbert's rescue? Do you realize that?"

"There is a great deal that I realize," Janet interrupted and the hardness in her voice matched that in his own for a moment. "I agree with Major Kingman's decision, Senator Hardin!"

For a moment, Mark Hardin stared at her as though he hadn't heard right. A faintly puzzled expression flickered across his face for a fleeting instant; then it was gone and arrogant impatience took its place once more.

"You're out of your head, my dear," he said, his voice patronizing. "You're tired. Go get your things together.

136

We'll spend the night at the hotel in Hagar. Tomorrow I'll send you home to wait for Gil back there."

"No," Janet told him, her head flung back. "I'll stay here. I was in the hotel in Hagar this afternoon. In a room alone with a man that they call Arco Blaine. I went there to try and undo some of the things that you have done out here, Senator Hardin. It is my fight as well as that of these other people—more, perhaps, for I have had a part in bringing this thing about, God help me!"

Mark Hardin blinked at her, swinging his heavy head slowly from side to side. "You went alone to this man in the hotel?" he asked thickly. "You? Gil's fiancée?"

There was pride in Janet as she faced him and, again, Frank Garland felt that warmth run through it. Coupled with a little shame for the doubts he had felt that afternoon.

"Yes. Alone," she said. "And I tell you, Senator Hardin, that I would go again and ten times again if it would do any good. I have learned that in this country you fight for what you want. I will tell you something more. If you persist in what you're trying to do, I will see that the world—your world—knows about it! I am not in the Army—yet—and I do not have to submit to the browbeatings of politicians, no matter how powerful they may be!"

That warmth was growing in Frank Garland. *She is wonderful,* he was thinking. *A soldier's woman!* Then memory that she belonged to Gil Hardin came again to strike him like a blow.

Mark Hardin was turning impatiently away now. He said, his voice flinty, "You will be good enough to have me driven to the hotel in Hagar, Major Kingman. I will communicate——"

He didn't finish for a shot, muffled by the night, suddenly pushed its echo into the room and Garland heard the sharp call, "Corporal of the guard! Post Number Two!" and reached the door in three long strides.

16. "A Leg Now. An Arm Later"

MONK WALTERS lay in his bunk, the blankets pulled around
his ears, while he waited impatiently for Taps. Presently,
he heard the eerie notes of the trumpet drifting lonesomely
off through the night. First Sergeant Jim Bestwood, lantern
swinging from his hand, came to make his bed check and
departed again and the long barrack room gradually became silent except for the tired noises which men make in
their sleep.

Corporal O'Garragh snored with a heavy seesaw of
sound. Trooper Bledsoe moaned softly as he tried to remember to keep from shutting his eyes as he squeezed off
on his carbine. Down at the far end of the room, next to
the washhouse door, a man turned uneasily and murmured,
"I never could figure that——I never could figure that
——" Monk Walters didn't know what it was that he
couldn't figure. Didn't care.

He waited for a long half-hour; then, fully dressed, he
slipped out of his bunk and, carrying his boots in his hand,
made his way softly out of the barracks and into the chill
of the night. A moon, its outline blurred a little by the mist,
was beginning to come up as Monk paused in the barrack's
shadow and slipped on his boots.

The night was quiet except for safe and familiar noises.
A dog's unconcerned barking down by Suds Row; the
sleepy hoot of an owl from a cottonwood in the creek's
bottom. The muffled sounds which the dozing troop horses
made in the stables. Monk Walters grinned a little with
satisfaction.

He went swiftly along behind the barracks and turned
back to skirt the stables. A faint trail here led down to the
willows and the cottonwoods of Cache Creek. Walking

swiftly he came presently to where the sentry path of Post Number Two crossed and waited here in the shadows.

Danny Jensen was on Post Number Two tonight, Monk knew, and Danny was a friend of his. Still, you didn't make it too hard on a man when he was doing you a favor— he'd give Danny ample time to get by. Danny passed, then, his boots clumping stolidly up and down on the hard packed path and Monk waited a few minutes longer for Danny to get to the far end of his post down by the commissary and the sutler's store. Then he slipped swiftly across and the shadows on the far side swallowed him.

The trail led steeply downward and he slithered along it until finally it flattened out along the creek bottom. Willows and alder and cottonwood made a thick shade here but enough of the moonlight came through to dapple the water a little as it made its whispered way over the stones. A hundred yards farther along, the creek made a bend to leave a flat bank beneath a screen of willows and Rita was waiting for him here.

She flung herself violently into Monk's arms.

"I was afraid that you weren't coming," she whispered after a little, her face pressed close against the rough cloth of his coat. "I couldn't have stood it, Monk, if you hadn't —not with you riding tomorrow."

He scowled into the moonlight at that, his usually facile tongue lacking an answer now, while he moved the palm of his hand up and down across the midnight black of her hair. There was something in the night which held both of them motionless and silent for a long moment. The soft rustle above them as the wind stirred the last leaves of the willows. The knowledge that tomorrow Monk would be gone.

Presently they sat on the bank's edge where they could look down on the winding ribbon of the creek and Monk put his coat about her shoulders for the nip of the wind was cold. She leaned against him and they talked in low voices of little things—inconsequential things—and each knew that the other was thinking of something else. A fish jumped in the creek and a frog made a low croaking and

139

far off, by Tumbleweed Butte, a coyote lent its mournful song to the night as the moon climbed higher into the sky.

Rita shivered a little and Monk tightened his arm about her. "He sounds so lonesome, Monk," she said in a small voice. "It's the way that I'll feel when you're gone."

"I'll be back, honey chile," Monk said, putting a forced flippancy into his voice. "I'm indestructible. Didn't you know that? I always come back."

"You're sure, Monk? Somehow, I've got a funny feeling this time. You'll be careful, won't you?"

"I'll hide behind a tree," Monk told her and bent swiftly to kiss her lips. "I'll sneak along underneath the belly of my horse if I see any Indians. Hell, kid, don't worry. There won't be no fight. We're just going out on a little ride to keep the animals in condition. I got the word."

"You always say that," Rita whispered. "But there have been fights—and everybody doesn't come back."

"I always come back, don't I?" Monk demanded practically. "Stop fretting—it'll spoil your looks and I wouldn't want that. Not ever." He stood up reluctantly; pulled her up close beside him and stood with his arms about her. "I've got to get back, kid," he said huskily. "You sure you can get back to town all right? I shouldn't have let you come out here like this."

"I'll be all right," she told him in a small voice. "It's not far. Monk?"

"Yeah?"

"You will be careful, won't you?"

"Sure," he answered in an absent voice, his face again twisted into a scowl in the faint moonlight. Somehow, he had never felt quite like this about Rita before, he was thinking. That sort of quivery feeling inside him—he hadn't felt that since he had said good-by to his mother in Springfield. It was like the grass and the elms and the soft voices of people walking home from church in the spring evenings.

He said, making his mind up swiftly, "My hitch has got a year to run yet. Then I'll get out and go home. My old man has got a shoeshop back there. He'll be glad to have me come in with him. Will you come back there with me, Rita?"

She was silent for a long moment and he could feel her shoulders quivering a little beneath his arms as she kept her face pressed close against his chest. Finally he turned her gently so that he could see her eyes and they were wide and tragic in the uncertain wash of the moonlight which filtered through the half-naked branches of the willows.

"Will you, Rita? I mean as my wife?"

She whispered, so low that he could barely hear it, "Oh, Monk! Monk!" and he knew what she was thinking.

He told her fiercely, "Look, kid, there's a hell of a lot of things that I've done in my life that I'd like to forget. We could forget together back in Springfield, couldn't we?"

She lifted her face suddenly; pressed her mouth passionately against his own in a long kiss. Then she said softly, "Come back to me, Monk," and was gone, running down Cache Creek through the mottled shadows.

Monk Walters waited until he could no longer see her, then turned slowly and started back to the post, his thoughts whirling in a crazy pattern in his head. He had never, in his twenty-three years, thought of anything like this before. But it was a nice thought. A nice thought.

His father's shop there on Westwood Street with its smell of leather and its whirring machines and his father, himself, peering over his half-spectacles—pipe in the corner of his mouth. And maybe a little house out on Long's Street with Rita, in a pretty dress and with her hair piled up on her head, waiting for him when he came home. And they'd forget all this.

Forget the reveilles in the cold dawns and the marches in the blistering noons. The water-and-feed; the boots-and-saddles; the trickling ripple as the trumpets sang the charge. Forget Fort Duncan and the dusty houses of Hagar. Yes, all that could be done.

He was wrapped in his thoughts so that he almost stumbled over the shadowy figure which crouched in the gloom where the trail started its climb out of the creek bottom and back to the level on which the fort lay. Monk Walters

141

jumped back, his hand instinctively reaching for the gun which should have been at his hip; swore under his breath when he found that it wasn't there. Some skulking Indian, he thought bitterly, and he was as naked of a weapon as was Moses in the bullrushes. Then Otto Fleigheimer's voice, shaky with fright, came to him through the uncertain light.

"Who's there?" it asked and Monk laughed shortly.

"Well!" he said. "It's the Dutch boy! What are you doing out here?"

He moved on forward until he could see Fleigheimer's face dimly through the trickle of moonlight.

"I could ask you the same thing," Fleigheimer countered sullenly. "I've got as much right to be out here as you have, I guess. Maybe more."

Monk Walters peered at him with narrowed eyes. The man wore a tortured, uncertain expression as he stood there fumbling at his belt with his big hands. "You wouldn't be going over the hill on the night before we go out on a scout, would you? They shoot people for that, Dutch boy. You'd better turn around and come back with me."

Fleigheimer shuffled his feet uncertainly. "I might as well be shot for a deserter as to be shot up on the Black-bird," he said in a low, strained voice. "I can feel it coming, Monk——"

"You don't feel nothing," Monk Walters told him roughly. "Come on or stay. I don't give a damn which."

He turned abruptly away and went on, climbing rapidly back up the trail. Otto Fleigheimer hesitated for a moment longer, then turned, too, and followed—hurrying to catch up. Together they waited for Danny Jensen to go by on his way to the far end of his post down by the commissary; then the two of them crossed swiftly and went on at a trot toward the barracks. They had reached the safety of the shadows by the stables when the sound of a shot punched out into the night and Danny Jensen's voice carried faintly to them against the lifting wind.

"Corporal of the guard! Post Number Two!"

"We were born under a lucky star, you and I," Monk Walters said, grinning as he led the way into the sleeping barracks. "There's going to be a fuss out there and we'd have never got back if we were still on the other side of that post now, Dutch boy. Stop worrying. Nothing can ever happen to us."

A moon had come out to push its feeble light through the haze as Frank Garland left Major Kingman's porch and started on a run toward the commissary where the shot had come from. Here Post Number Two led along the high bank which tumbled down into Cache Creek and it would be here that a man would come if he were trying to get to Whitewater Charley.

Garland rounded the commissary's corner and saw a dim figure break from the shadows and run for the shelter of the sutler's store. He called, "Halt!" with a hard command in his voice but the running man went on and was swallowed again by the shadows.

It was Arco Blaine, Garland thought. It had to be.

He moved on, his gun ready in his hand, and called then, "Come on out, Blaine." A spit of orange fire, coming from the corner of the sutler's store, was all that answered him. Off to the left he could hear the pound of running footsteps as the corporal of the guard came with the first relief behind him.

Bitter anger suddenly racked Garland. That man over there in the shadows was the one who had caused all of this. The beaten look on Caleb Kingman's face. The sadness in Marjory Kingman's eyes. Benson, Jarvis—all of the rest.

He called roughly, "I'm coming after you, Arco," and started forward, his gun lifted and ready.

Then Arco Blaine's voice called from the shadows, "Get back, Frank! Damn you, get back!"

He paid no attention to that, going on with a steady stride, and then an orange flower again made a fleeting splash against the sutler's wall and Garland heard the whisper of the bullet as it went by and he laid his bullets in there with a cold precision, feeling the solid jump of the Colt as it hit the crotch of his hand. The echoes of the gun fire rolled up into the night and a man said, "Ahhhhh," in a long sigh and then the night was quiet again.

Jensen, the sentry on Number Two, came pounding up then, his carbine held ready and, behind him, Garland could hear the others as they got near. From the left, Major Kingman called out, "Who is it, Frank? Are you all right?" and Garland said, "Arco Blaine, I think," and went on toward the shadows with his gun covering the crumpled figure which he made out dimly on the ground.

He had been right, he thought as he stood over Arco Blaine and slowly slid the revolver back into its holster. He had known that the man would come. The corporal of the guard came up, panting then, and Garland said curtly, "Take your relief and beat the willows down by the creek for more skulkers, corporal," and the men wheeled and went on off at a trot.

Garland knelt in the dust, wind blowing cold against his face as he turned Arco Blaine over. The man still lived, his eyes staring sardonically up in the faint moonlight.

He said in a whisper which bubbled a little in his throat, "Nice shooting, Frank. You were always good with a gun."

"Where are you hit?" Garland asked, his voice expressionless, and Blaine thought of that for the space of a half-dozen breaths and then said, "It doesn't matter. It's bad enough."

The sergeant of the guard came then, bringing a lantern which laid shifting patterns of light across the ground as he ran, and Garland said harshly, "Let's have that light here," and placed the lantern down. He began to unbutton Blaine's coat and pull the shirt away. Blaine stared up at him with the cynicism dark and bitter in his eyes.

"You're wasting your time, Frank," he whispered hoarsely. "Can't you call your shots better than that?"

Major Kingman came trotting up now with Mark Hardin and Janet Davenport behind him and Garland waved them impatiently back as he pulled the shirt away and probed with gentle fingers. There was a damp hole low in Blaine's

144

side and the husky rattle of the man's breathing told him that Arco Blaine was done for. He felt no regret. No triumph. Nothing at all.

Blaine sensed that and he twisted his mouth into its old, mocking grin. "You have won, friend Frank," he said slowly, as though he searched deep for each word. "I am sorry for that—I meant it to be the other way."

"Don't talk," Frank Garland told him in a flat voice. "Sergeant, get a litter."

"Not necessary," Blaine said, his whisper rising faintly against the cold buffet of the wind. The flickering light of the lantern made a yellow wash across his dark, saturnine face. "There is one thing in my life that I am sorry for, Frank."

"Don't talk," Garland told him again in a rough voice. He knew what Arco Blaine was about to say and he didn't want to hear it. "There is nothing to talk about."

"Martha," Blaine whispered. "I am sorry about Martha, Frank. I am not sorry about anything else at all."

Garland's fingers shook a little as he pulled Blaine's shirt back across his chest to keep the wind away. He said harshly, "Leave Martha out of this, Blaine," and then his fingers touched the folded paper in the pocket of Blaine's coat and he pulled it out and looked at it in the lantern's smoky light. Blood made a dark smear across the paper.

"My commission, Frank," Arco Blaine said sardonically, breath rattling deep in his throat again. "Give it to the senator. He can keep it as a souvenir——"

Garland turned his head a little, saw Mark Hardin standing silently there, his face strained in the moonlight, and held the blood-stained paper toward him. Mark Hardin made no move to take it and finally Major Kingman picked it out of Garland's fingers—looked down at it and then turned his attention back to the man on the ground.

"We'd better get him to the hospital, Frank," he said slowly but Garland shook his head. Arco Blaine saw that gesture and smiled again, working his lips into a painful grimace beneath the thin line of his mustache.

"Frank is more of a realist than you are, major," he said and Janet, watching, knew that each word was torture to the man who lay there. Sudden pity welled up in her and she started to move forward but Frank Garland waved her back.

"He needs no comfort for his dying," he said in a hard voice. "Let Senator Hardin comfort him, if he can."

Arco Blaine seemed to take some faint pleasure in that for the corners of his mouth quirked up a little and his eyes sought those of the big man who stood there behind Frank Garland's shoulder, looking down. Blaine's faint smile deepened, became more cynical.

"You are the only one who will win in this thing, senator," he said haltingly. "And that is funny because you are as bad as I am—worse, I think, for you do what you do for greed—while I had only ambition. And hate."

He fell silent for a moment and none of the others spoke now, held mute by the intensity of the dying man's voice. A coyote sung out lonesomely from the pale shadow of the hills; the wind came again to wail around the corner of the sutler's store. The corporal of the guard returned with his relief from beating the willows down along the creek bottom; stood a little way off from the knot of people waiting there in the lantern's glow. The corporal's face was impassive. He had seen better men than Arco Blaine die.

Blaine coughed—a choking *rale* of sound; then the fit passed and the faint smile came back again as Arco kept his attention fixed on Mark Hardin.

"You will get what you want, senator," Arco Blaine was going on. "You commissioned me to stir the Indians up. I stirred them up. I sold them whiskey and guns. I persuaded them to leave the reservation. That was what you wanted——"

Mark Hardin said, "Stop!" in a hoarse voice but Arco Blaine paid no attention as he talked on.

"But one thing you didn't figure on, senator—they got your son. After I'm dead, they'll send him back to you. A leg now. An arm later——"

Mark Hardin said again, "Stop! For God's sake, stop!"

146

The sardonic satisfaction deepened in Arco Blaine's face as he rolled his head a little so that he could see Mark Hardin better.

"I could tell Whitewater Charley how to stop that, senator," he said with his voice suddenly clear. "Just a word from me—but I will not give that word——"

His voice died away, whistling a little in his throat, and Frank Garland straightened and looked down and wondered at the warped hate which could make a man choose this way to die. But Arco Blaine was not yet through for he turned his eyes now until they found Janet, standing with Major Kingman's arm thrown protectingly around her.

"You are lucky," Arco Blaine whispered hoarsely. "Gil Hardin was not good enough for you. I am glad that he will not have you for he would have given you nothing but—hurt. And Frank Garland is too big a fool to see the things that I see——"

Mark Hardin pushed himself forward now and Garland saw the change that had come over the big man's face. There was an agony there and an indecision and a terrible awareness. "Blaine," he said in a broken voice, "you can't do this thing! Send some word to Broken Feather about Gil——"

"No," Arco Blaine said and died.

17. Through Fort Duncan's Gate

THE FIRST FAINT STIRRINGS OF DAWN came with a gray and lowering sky and the wind blowing steadily out of the north. Wind which no longer had anything of autumn in it; wind which was biting cold and which carried the smell of snow on its breath. It whipped the dust across the parade ground, still but dimly seen through the last fringes of the night. It harried the tumbleweeds caught in the brush along the lip of Cache Creek and it rattled the windows of the barracks where K prepared to ride.

The company had been astir for two hours now. Pots still banged with a tinny racket in the kitchen where the cooks had fried bacon and flapjacks and boiled coffee; off by the stables, lanterns winked like uneasy fireflies in the chill morning. The numbing, uncertain depression of an hour that was too early hung over half-awakened men who moved about slowly, life still torpid in their bodies, as they cursed at their tasks.

Lieutenant Oglethorpe Henderson came into the orderly room, buckling his pistol belt about his waist as he came, and Frank Garland looked up—worried a little as he saw the thinness of Henderson's face and the pinched look about his mouth and nose. Damn it, Thorpe shouldn't be going on this trip, he thought irritably. That old wound had had too little time to heal.

He said, "Morning, Thorpe. You sure that you want to go along on this rat race? You don't have to."

Oglethorpe Henderson gave him an easy grin. "I'll go along, Frank," he said in a light voice. "I need the exercise —getting fat as a hog sitting behind that desk at headquarters," and Garland's mouth tipped up a little in answer. He was vastly fond of this lanky lieutenant who habitually rode at his right hand.

"Mary give you permission?" he asked. "I don't want her after my scalp, Thorpe."

"Sure. Sure," Oglethorpe Henderson told him. "She told me that she'd leave me for a better man if I didn't go along. She's got sewing to do—I'd get in the way if I stayed home."

And both of them knew that was a lie. Mary Henderson would be going about her morning chores now with that set, pinched look on her face while she waited for the steady clump-clump of the horses as K moved out. She would cry a little after Thorpe left her—not much and never where he could see—but she would not lift a hand to try and keep him from going, Frank Garland knew.

He said, the lightness in his tone matching that of his lieutenant, "If she's looking for a better man, I'll get my application in today, boy."

Oglethorpe Henderson liked that for he grinned and went on across the orderly room to pick up his saddle roll. "Nasty wind this morning," he said. "Going to storm, I think."

Garland nodded. "Toronto says that that old bullet in his leg is kicking up. That's a sure sign."

The orderly room door opened to let in a gust of the rising wind, and Mark Hardin came in with Sergeant Jim Bestwood following angrily at his heels. Bestwood shook his head at Garland and said in a flinty voice, "This man insisted on seeing the captain. I couldn't keep him out."

"It's all right, Jim," Garland told him evenly. "Go on about your chores. I'll handle this," and turned an impersonal regard on Mark Hardin.

The older man wore a buffalo coat and his trousers were stuffed into heavy boots and there were gauntlets on his hands. Dressed to ride, Garland reflected curiously. Now, what in the hell was this going to be? Then memory of last night came back to flatten his mouth out into a thin line.

"Well, Senator Hardin?" he asked curtly.

149

Mark Hardin stood just inside the door and looked back at him. "Good morning, captain," he said in a flat voice. "I'm going with you on this expedition."

"No!" Garland told him, putting a hard finality into the words. "Perhaps you have the power to appoint and relieve the commanding officers of this post, Senator Hardin. I do not know. You do not have the power to give me orders here in Company K. I will not permit that. If necessary, I will have you escorted back across the parade ground at the point of a gun. Do you understand?"

For a moment the two stood, eyes clashing, while Oglethorpe Henderson made an interested spectator by the window. It was Mark Hardin who broke first under the pressure, turning his gaze away, and Frank Garland felt a little thread of surprise run through him for he suddenly perceived again the anguish that had come into Mark Hardin's face last night as he had watched Arco Blaine die. An uncertainty. A lostness—almost a petition now. Expressions which were alien to this man so long accustomed to dictating to others. To having his own way unopposed.

"Major Kingman is still in command, captain," Mark Hardin said slowly, no anger in his voice now. "He has agreed that I will ride with the column—if you will allow it. I am asking for that permission now. I have a right to go."

Anger burned suddenly in Frank Garland then as he made a chopping gesture with his hand. "You have no rights at all in K Company," he said, whipping his words at the other. "The mission on which we are starting is not play. I do not intend to make that mission more difficult by hampering myself with a civilian unaccustomed to the hard riding—and fighting—that we can expect. Particularly, I do not mean to hamper myself with you, Senator Hardin!"

Mark Hardin shook his head a little, no resentment showing in his face as he put out a placating hand. "I am tougher than you may think, captain," he said, his voice getting a little thick and slurred now. "I can stand the pace. And, should I not be able to stand it, you can leave me

150

behind. But I've got to go with you! Can't you see that? I've got to be there when you find Gilbert——"

His voice trailed away and Garland scowled at him, his anger suddenly gone now and puzzled lines wrinkling his forehead. "I don't understand you," he said finally. "Last night I thought I understood you too well. Now, I'm not sure."

"Last night I thought that I understood myself, Captain Garland," Mark Hardin said slowly. He paused for a little and allowed his eyes to run over the Spartan appointments of the small room which was Garland's office. The makeshift filing cabinet; the rough table which served as a desk, bare now of its papers. The gear—sabers and cartridge belts and canteens—which hung on the walls. The company guidon in one corner. Then he turned his attention somberly back to Frank Garland, "Gilbert is my only son, captain. That should make things clear, I think."

And Garland remembered then the thing that Arco Blaine had promised last night before he had died out there by the sutler's store. "You will get him back, senator. A leg at one time—an arm at another." And felt a sudden revulsion.

Hell, what did it matter after all if Senator Mark Hardin accompanied K? Maybe it was one of the rights that the man had. He swung around toward Oglethorpe Henderson, still lounging by the window and gestured briefly.

"See that Senator Hardin has a good mount, Thorpe," he said quietly. "I'm going across the way to report to the major now. As soon as I get back, we'll ride."

A lantern hung in the middle of the stable, its light making a yellow splash against the log walls and flooding over the hardpacked ground. It was warm in here, steamy with the heat of the animals and acrid with stable smells. Trumpeter Monk Walters whistled softly between his teeth as he saddled, paying no attention to the ill-natured grumble which went on around him as men tossed McClellan saddles onto the backs of the edgy troop horses, buckled rolls and slid carbines into boots, and led out into the gray chill of the morning.

Memory of last night was still strong in Monk and he was thinking of his father's shop in Westwood Street and of how green the grass had used to look back in Springfield, Massachusetts, in June. Corporal O'Garragh came by, leading his big, raw-boned sorrel and gave Monk an irritated glance as he passed.

"What in the hell are you so happy about?" he demanded morosely. "This is not the time of the morning to whistle."

"I'm the cheerful sort," Monk Walters said, reaching under his horse's belly to catch the swinging cinch. "I'm the sort that looks at the bright side of things, Mister O'Garragh."

"You'll be looking at the bright underside of a spade before this shindig is over," Corporal O'Garragh told him crossly and went on out into the morning.

Monk Walters yanked the cinch tight; slapped his horse affectionately on the neck and then was aware that Otto Fleigheimer had come softly up in the uncertain light that the lantern made. Fleigheimer's stolid face was not quite so sullen this morning, Monk Walters saw, and there was a faint diffidence in his manner as he stood there.

Monk said, "Howdy, Dutch boy. And how do you find yourself on this lovely, lovely morning?"

Fleigheimer shifted his feet nervously and looked away. Finally brought his attention back to Monk. "I just wanted to ask you," he said vaguely. "You know about last night, Monk?"

"Yep," Monk said. "I know about last night. Why?"

"You remember what you said when we got back to barracks?" Fleigheimer persisted stubbornly. "That thing about you and me being born under a lucky star and nothing could happen to us?"

Monk Walters straightened and squinted his eyes a little as he looked at the other across the top of the McClellan saddle. He said finally, "Sure, I remember, Dutch boy. What's bothering you?"

152

He saw the relief which slowly spread across Fleigheimer's heavy face and grinned then as he understood. The Dutch boy was clinging to that idea of luck as they got ready to ride—well, what the hell? A man had to cling to something.

"I just wanted to be sure, is all," Fleigheimer mumbled. "Much obliged, Monk." He turned away down the lantern-lit length of the stable, walking with steps which were surer now.

Monk called after him, "Stick with me, boy, and you'll be all right. Just stick with me," and grinned again as he went back to strapping the gear on his saddle.

The wind had a bitter slap against his face as Frank Garland went across the parade ground toward Major Kingman's quarters. The unseasonable heat of the last two weeks was bound to bring a vicious change of weather down on their heads now, he was thinking. October in this country could be trickier than a tinhorn dealer's shuffle. Blistering summer heat one day; a howling blizzard, the next. Well, K had ridden in blizzards before.

Major Caleb Kingman was waiting for him in the same room where they had talked last night. The old man looked gray and tired in the early light, Frank thought as he saluted and waited for the major to speak.

The major said then, "You're ready to move out, Frank?"

Garland nodded. "We're ready, sir."

Major Kingman lifted a hand to touch his chin; turned his eyes to the window where the wind was driving grits of sand against the glass. "Bad weather," he said slowly. "I regret that I have to send you into it. It will not be pleasant going, Frank. Not pleasant."

Garland murmured, a little amusement in his eyes, "Since when has soldiering been pleasant, major?" and Major Kingman's lips quirked a little at that.

"Not within my memory," he said drily and Garland, watching, knew that the other's spirits had lifted a little. He thought: *It's always a hell of a lot easier to go than to*

153

stay. I know how the Old Man feels. I wouldn't trade with him. Then Major Kingman asked in a gentle voice, "Senator Hardin has seen you?"

"Yes," Frank told him. "I have given him permission to go with us, sir."

"I would not have ordered you to do it," Major Kingman said thoughtfully. "Still, I am glad you consented. I can understand his feelings."

Garland said, "Yes," in a noncommittal voice and Major Kingman allowed the subject to die.

He moved slowly across the room and said then, "I have hopes that you can scatter Feather's band—bring Feather back as a prisoner. If you can do that, the rest of his band will drift on back to the reservation, particularly if the weather turns bad. That will avert any further uprising."

"I'm counting on that," Garland replied soberly. "We'll try to catch Feather by surprise—just at daybreak, if we can. Moving with a small, fast column should make that possible and this weather will help. We'll hit them hard with everything we've got. There's no point in using half measures in this thing, sir. Too many half measures have already been used."

"Yes," Major Kingman murmured. "Too many half measures. I have the fullest confidence in your judgment, Frank."

Garland let that go by, frowning a little as he weighed the factors of this thing in his mind. "Whitewater Charley is our ace in the hole," he said finally. "Without him we could search for weeks in the hills without ever finding where Feather and his band are holed up. As it is, we'll head straight for this place that the breed has told us about. We should stand a good chance of hitting the Sioux before they know we're about."

Major Kingman nodded his agreement. "It is a reasonable hope," he murmured. "Do you think that Lieutenant Hardin is still alive, Frank?"

Garland shrugged. "No telling. I think that it's no worse than an even chance. We'll find out."

Major Kingman sighed a little and came around the

table to drop a hand on Garland's shoulder. "Good luck, Frank," he said. "Don't take any more chances than you have to."

Garland smiled as he stepped back and saluted. "No more than you've taken a hundred times, sir," he said and half turned away.

Major Kingman returned the smile and the salute. "The taking of chances is a thing that runs in us, I guess, Frank. But make them good chances."

Garland nodded and moved on toward the door and then Marjory Kingman came swiftly in from the back of the house, her hands outstretched and her eyes bright. "You were not going off without saying good-by, Frank?" she asked softly.

He said, "Never that, Maggie," and bent down and kissed her lightly on the cheek and then swung away to go through the front door and out into the wind again.

Day had come now with a gray sullenness so that the barracks, the stables, the commissary, the sutler's store stood out in a drab panorama before his eyes. A cheerless settlement here huddling itself against the prairie. An outpost.

And yet there was a dignity in that picture spread before him, he thought as he paused on the porch of the major's quarters for a moment. A quiet assurance which had been brought here and planted by the men and the women who peopled these far places. For they were the Army.

Not the fat and lackadaisical Army which sprawled amid the salons of Washington. They were the Indian-fighting Army and that made a difference. For the mistress whom they served was a hard and exacting one and she gave little and required much, but still they would follow the bright glow of duty and service which illumed her face. And they would listen to her voice and obey although the why of that was not always clear.

Garland shrugged the thoughts away—a man should not think too much out here. Not when he was about to ride after the Sioux. It was enough that he concerned himself

155

with the chores immediately at hand. They were ample to keep him busy.

K was beginning to lead out from the stables, he saw as he hitched at his gun belt and stepped down from the porch. He could hear the grumble of the troopers' voices coming to him faintly against the wind as he set off with a long stride.

Then Janet Davenport called to him softly. "Frank!" she said and Garland stopped abruptly and turned. She was standing at the corner of the quarters wrapped closely against the bite of the wind and with her face questioning in the early light as she turned it toward him.

He hesitated for a moment; then went to her. He said, "You should not be out at this hour——" and then stopped, a little puzzled by what he saw in her eyes. Concern was there and foreboding, he thought, and why should that be?

"You're going now, Frank," she said slowly, lifting her face to his own. It was a statement; not a question. "I had to say good-by to you. To wish you luck."

It seemed a natural thing now that she should use his given name. He stood close to her, looking down and her eyes did not waver as they met his own and he was suddenly aware of the faint perfume of her. And Frank Garland, looking at her, knew with a terrible desolation that she was a desirable woman and that he wanted her for his own. Bitterness run through him in a hot stream as he remembered that she belonged to Gil Hardin.

Well, that was that.

"We'll find Gil, Janet," he said, keeping his voice flat and expressionless. "I'm sorry things have worked out in the way they have. It could not be helped."

"I know that, Frank," she told him in a sober voice. "I know many things now that I didn't know before. You'll be careful?"

Careful so that young Gil Hardin would return to her, Garland thought sardonically. "It is a habit of mine to be careful, Miss Davenport," he told her stiffly.

He saw the swift darkening of her eyes as she stepped

156

forward to place a hand on his arm. "I like 'Janet' better, Frank," she said, her voice so low that he scarcely heard it. "Too much has happened—don't let anything happen to you."

For a moment Frank Garland thought back to last night and the thing that Arco Blaine had said. *"Frank Garland is too big a fool."* A sudden impulse urged him to take this woman into his arms; to leave with at least a remembrance of her kiss on his mouth. A man deserved that. Then he shoved the thought angrily out of his mind.

"Time to ride, Miss Davenport," he said roughly and gave her a half-salute and wheeled away into the wind.

Janet stood looking after him as he went. *He is going to bring Gil back to me,* she was thinking with a lump making an aching knot in her breast. *And I don't want Gil. I want you, Frank and you won't come back!*

K was mounted as Garland reached the stables. Oglethorpe Henderson saluted with an easy lift of his hand and said, "Everything ready to roll, Frank," and Garland nodded his understanding. Mark Hardin was there, bulky in his buffalo coat; troopers, similarly bundled against the growing coldness of the wind, gentled their restless mounts. Toronto Peters sat dumpily on his horse, jaws working on a quid and his eyes sleepy.

Another scout. Another fight. Another filing through the main gate, Toronto Peters was thinking phlegmatically. He'd seen it before and it was all the same to him.

Garland stepped to the bay which Trumpeter Monk Walters was holding for him. Made an unhurried last inspection of his saddlebags and then swung up into the saddle. He lifted an arm; called, "Column of twos—walk —Ho!" and let his arm drop and they moved slowly across the hard packed earth as the gray dawn began to lift in front of them.

The guard was drawn up to pass them through the gate and they rode on, men sullen and crotchety in the morning. A girl stood there, Garland noted absently. It was Annie

157

Helfron from Suds Row and she turned her head to search the column with a swift and pleading look.

He turned a little in his saddle; saw Trooper Fraley a third of the way back along the column. The boy had spotted Annie there by the gate and there was something in his face which moved Garland, a forlornness—as though the world had suddenly moved too fast for young Paul Melrose Fraley and now it was too late to do the things that he had meant to do.

Garland said to Sergeant Brecheen, riding at right guide, "Go back and fall out young Fraley. Tell him to rejoin the column in five minutes," and Brecheen grinned and said, "Yes, sir. He'll fight the better for it," and wheeled his horse.

18. Approach March

FRANK GARLAND led the column down the steep bank to the crossing of Cache Creek and into the trail on the other side. The splashing of the horses made a clear, musical sound in the quiet morning and then they were headed north with Fort Duncan falling away behind them as they rode.

Blood began to run warmly again in Frank now as his muscles slackened and eased themselves to the fit of the saddle. The bay, made lively by the cold, danced a little between his legs and Garland gentled him with a big hand while his spirits began to lift. This was the thing that a man was made for, he thought—to ride at the head of other men with a good horse beneath him and the wind blowing in his face and the trail stretching ahead.

He turned a little in his saddle to look back. The apathy of early morning still held the men, he saw, but didn't worry. That would wear off as the morning mists began to lift a little; the rough banter would start. For he knew these men of K; knew all of them. They had ridden often together.

Corporal O'Garragh back there with his red face set stiffly now against the cold. McNair and Cameron and Johnson and the Dutchman, Schmidt. Young Fraley with his head held high now and a new and eager light in his eyes. First Sergeant Jim Bestwood coming soberly at the tail of the column. Good men, all of them.

Senator Mark Hardin rode back there beside Jim Bestwood, heavy shoulders hunched forward a little and his hands resting on the pommel of his saddle. The way that he swung with his horse's gait showed that he had ridden much before and that was good. You didn't abandon a man—even a senator, Frank Garland thought with a faint flash of amusement—out here in Indian country and he would have had trouble on his hands had Hardin not been

159

able to keep up. He swung back to the front again and gave his attention to the country which lay ahead.

Another column. Another scout.

Presently he turned in his saddle; lifted an arm and sung out, "Trot—Ho!" and the company picked up the pace, the men becoming more alive as the movement warmed their blood.

They went on, taking the trail which led up Cache Creek, with gear jangling and thumping now—horses blowing in the cold. Shod hooves rang against the stones and the low murmur of talk started among the troopers. This was the way that he liked it, Garland was thinking. Dust making a faint banner above them and air like wine in their throats.

K was on its way.

At a little after eight o'clock they crossed the divide at the headwaters of Cache Creek and angled down toward the cottonwoods and adlers of Fourth of July Fork which would take them to the Blackbird where Gil Hardin had fought his abortive skirmish. Sun had not broken through the leaden clouds which hung low in the sky and the day was gray and unfriendly.

At nine it started to snow; by ten the air was full of the clinging flakes, driven by the wind in a slanting curtain. The going began to get slick underfoot and Garland held the column to a walk as they angled back and forth down through the timber.

He halted them at noon where the Fourth of July joins the Blackbird. There was a long flat here, sparsely timbered, and the company dismounted to rest the horses and make coffee and eat the cold sandwiches which they had brought along in their saddlebags. The snow was falling faster now.

When he had finished eating, Monk Walters made his brown paper cigarette, carefully licking the flap and smoothing its edge with his fingers. He set it alight and leaned his back against a rock as Corporal O'Garragh came and hunkered down beside him. Around him were the sounds born in a column at a halt. The uneasy stamp of horses; the lazy talk of men, just fed and satisfied to be free of the discipline of the barracks again. Fifty yards away, Fourth of July Fork brawled whitely as it spilled over the rocks, and the wind made a gentle murmur as it pulled at the nearly leafless branches of the cottonwoods. Monk Walters savored his cigarette with satisfaction.

Monk said, looking out of the corners of his eyes, "I do declare, Mister O'Garragh, Trooper Fraley looks just like he had had the canary for breakfast. Would that red-cheeked Annie Helfron have anything to do with that, you suppose?"

"Why now," Corporal O'Garragh answered with an elaborate unconcern, "I guess I wouldn't know anything about that, Trumpeter Walters. I'm not a ladies man, myself."

"I noticed that," Monk Walters retorted cheerfully. "Hey, Fraley, Annie give you a lock of her hair?"

Trooper Fraley, sitting a little at one side and busy with his own thoughts, blushed a painful red but said nothing and Sergeant Brecheen, passing by, said with a heavy good humor, "Let the boy alone, Monk. No good woman would look twice at *you!*"

Monk Walters let that go as he gave Fraley a bright glance which was not unfriendly and turned his attention back to O'Garragh again. "Why does a man soldier anyway, O'Garragh?" he asked. "Can you give me an answer to that?"

"To get rich," O'Garragh told him and threw back his red head to roar with laughter. Monk Walters paid no attention. The levity had gone out of his lean, handsome face now and he was staring somberly at the white foam which Fourth of July Fork made as it battered down against the rocks.

"It ain't because he wants a uniform," he said thoughtfully, speaking half to himself. "We have got marching lodges back home in Springfield, Massachusetts, that have got a lot prettier uniforms than we got."

Corporal O'Garragh grunted, "What's eating on you, Monk? Let it go," but Walters paid no attention as he reached a hand up to wipe the snow from his face.

"And it ain't because the Army feeds you so good," he went on reflectively. "Because it don't. And it ain't because you lead such an interesting life. What in hell is interesting about pokin' around in a storm like this?"

"You talk like a guardhouse lawyer," Tim O'Garragh said disgustedly. "What's on your mind?"

Monk Walters shrugged his shoulders, suddenly discarding his soberness as a man discards an old shoe. "I was just thinking that I'd ought to settle down, Mister O'Garragh," he said, grinning. "Lead the good life. You got any suggestions?"

"Sure," O'Garragh told him, a little relieved at the change in the other's mood. "Join the church. Or maybe you could get into a nunnery some place. Loan me your makings—I got mine all buttoned inside my coat."

Monk Walters passed the papers and the sack of tobacco across. "Just call me 'Sutler Walters' from now on," he grunted. "How can you get so lazy, you fat Mick?"

Farther along, Frank Garland and Toronto Peters talked with Whitewater Charley, while Jim Bestwood stood by and watched with suspicious eyes. He didn't trust breeds. Garland was saying tightly, "You're in a spot, Charley. Blaine is dead and, if you cross us up now, you'll have nobody to get you out of trouble. On the other hand, if you play square with us, I'll recommend that the Army turn you loose when we get back. You've got a choice—but not very much of a choice, Charley."

Whitewater Charley stared sullenly into the falling snow; then shrugged his skinny shoulders. "I won't try to lead you wrong, captain," he said, his face settling into morose, hopeless lines. "I'm done for in this country anyway. Like I told you, Feather will go back into this place that the Injuns call 'Hole-That-Hides' beyond the Kenesaw. He's probably already there—it's a hard place to get into."

"But you know the way in?"

Whitewater Charley nodded glumly, sitting cross-legged in the snow. "Through Kenesaw canyon. Only way in that I ever heard about. Broken country all around the place."

Garland nodded and turned away, saying to Jim Bestwood, "Keep a close eye on him, Jim. He's our map on this trip."

Mark Hardin was standing a little way off, staring somberly at the snow settling into the creek. Garland hesitated for a moment; then turned sharply and went over to him. Again, he had the feeling that this was a different man from the one who had stood in Major Kingman's living room last night, beating the others down with the furious anger of his words. Mark Hardin turned eagerly as Garland came up.

"You have found out something from the half-breed?" he asked quickly, with a sudden hope creeping into his voice. "He has told you something about Gil?"

Garland shook his head, a little sorry for this man now. "He knows nothing, Senator Hardin," he said slowly. "He has been giving us more details as to the way in to where he thinks that Feather's band is. Nothing more."

Mark Hardin said, his voice expressionless again, "I see. Thank you, captain," and turned away toward the horses.

They forded the Blackbird early in the afternoon and angled up through broken country toward the watershed which divided the Blackbird and the Kenesaw. Rough country here, broken by gullies and slippery in the falling snow. It was necessary to halt the column often to breathe the horses and good humor was going out of the men now as the fatigue of ten hours of steady riding bit into them.

It was late in the afternoon when they crossed the divide and began to angle down toward water again. Still wilder country here. Firs, somber beneath their hoods of snow, began to dot the slopes. A deer broke from cover in front of the column and went away in graceful bounds.

The company camped that night in sparse timber well up the Kenesaw. Three inches of snow lay on the ground and although the snowfall had stopped now there was something in the sough of the wind which warned that there was worse weather still to come. Toronto Peters, drifting by in the dusk, stopped to squat by the tiny fire where Garland and Henderson made coffee and cooked bacon.

"I been in this country for a long time, Frank," Toronto said. "I can smell weather. An', when I ain't smellin' it, that condemned bullet in my leg lets me know about it. Both of 'em are puttin' up quite a holler now."

Lieutenant Henderson got to his feet, dusting the snow from his breeches and went off for more firewood and Frank Garland sipped his coffee—bitter and red hot— from the lip of his tin bucket; absently passed the bucket across to Toronto. "Both of what?" he asked, busy with his own thoughts.

All day, memory of Janet's face—as he had last seen her standing there beside Major Kingman's quarters—had ridden with him. He had tried to push it away but it had returned; watched him from across the red coals now.

"Both my nose an' my knee," Toronto Peters said crossly in answer to the question. "What's the matter, Frank? You ain't seein' spooks, are you?"

Garland shrugged and reluctantly brought his mind back to the present. To this cold camp up here above the Kenesaw. Toronto was right—he had been seeing spooks. For the thoughts that he had been thinking were ghost thoughts which could never come true. Not in this world. He put them away.

"Have some more coffee, Pete," he said roughly. "All right. What do you think the weather'll do?"

"It's got the smell of a blizzard," Toronto Peters told him sourly. "If it was me, I'd say to hell with the Injuns and to hell with Gil Hardin and hightail it back to Fort Duncan tomorrow morning."

"It's not you, Pete," Frank Garland told him gently then. "Tomorrow we go on."

"There's a pigheadedness that runs in the Army," Toronto mused. "I used to think that they taught it at West Point but I ain't so sure since I've known you, Frank. You got it, too, an' I never heard of you learning your soldiering at West Point."

"I learned my soldiering at seventeen in the Army of the

164

Potomac," Garland said, grinning a little. "Ever hear of it? You talk too much, Pete."

"I do, for a fact," Toronto Peters agreed placidly. "Reason I married a squaw, Frank. I do the talkin'—she does the work. Comes out all even that way."

The guard awoke K at five-thirty, kicking cursing troopers out of their snow-dusted blankets and presently the camp came alive again. Same old pattern. Water and feed. Coffee gulped hurriedly to wash down bacon and hardtack softened in the bacon's grease. Then the creak of saddles and the jangle of gear and the ill-humored sneezing of horses as men mounted in the gray dawn.

It was midafternoon when the valley began to narrow, blocked here and there by boulders—big as houses—which had rolled down from the walls above. An hour later they came to the canyon into which the Kenesaw boiled, mad and brawling; Garland halted the column here and gave orders for a camp.

He said to Henderson, "You're in charge, Thorpe, until I get back. Pete and I will scout on down the canyon while there's still a little daylight left. We'll take the breed with us and Walters will go along as messenger."

"I could go," Henderson said and Garland saw that his face was more pinched and lean after two days of riding. He brushed the idea away.

"My job," he said shortly. "Have the men get their supper but don't unsaddle. We'll be moving on tonight if I find what I'm looking for."

He led the way out, the three others following him in single file, and presently K was lost in the haze behind them. The going was bad and grew steadily worse as they worked their way deeper into the Kenesaw's canyon; after an hour it was necessary to dismount and lead the horses. Walls rose sheer on either side and the river roared by on their left, flinging itself against the buttresses which held it in check.

A hell of a place for an ambush, Garland thought, and hoped that his figuring had been right and that weather

165

would keep the Sioux snug in their lodges for the next twenty hours. If it didn't, things could be bad. Really bad!

It was almost dark when the walls began to open again, spreading out into a "V" which let the last of the day's light in. The four mounted again here and went cautiously on. Then the Kenesaw made a bend, swinging around a steep bluff, and they followed it around for a quarter of a mile until Whitewater Charley lifted a hand beside Garland and grunted a hoarse warning.

"Hole-that-Hides up ahead," he said.

"How far?" Garland asked him and the breed held up two fingers. " 'bout two mile, I think."

Garland nodded and they went on until a screen of dark trees hid the opening land from their sight and here Garland dismounted them again, leaving Walters to hold the horses while he started on through the thick timber on foot. Toronto Peters and the breed followed along behind. A finger of ridge ran down toward the water here and they climbed it in the last of the day's light and lay, belly down, on the crest where they could peer into the deepening haze below.

"Hole-that-Hides," Whitewater Charley mumbled under his breath. Toronto Peters whistled softly.

"Frank, there's a hell of a lot of Injuns down there! A hell of a lot!"

Too many, Frank Garland thought soberly as he adjusted his glasses. Below them, there was a bowl ringed by the hills and dotted with firs and—dark against the white carpet of the snow—there were the lodges of a big band. Sixty of them, at least. Probably more. That could mean a hundred braves. Long odds, Garland thought, while he wondered with a vaguely detached indifference if young Gil Hardin was in one of those lodges.

He swung his glasses to the left, saw trampled snow at the mouth of a small feeder canyon and guessed that the horse herd would be hidden there. Searching the ground in front, he made his plan of attack. Sergeant Brecheen would move to the left with a squad; stampede the horses down through the camp first. He would hold the rest of K here behind the ridge. At the right moment take it slamming in. A simple plan but as good as any—that was the way that it would be.

"I've seen enough," he grunted to Toronto Peters. "I'm going back now to bring the company up. You stay here and keep an eye on the village, Pete."

"Going to be awful cold," Toronto said dolefully. "I wish that I was back with my old woman right now, Frank."

Garland gave him a flat stare; then grinned a little wryly. "There's sixty-five other men, counting me, who'd just as soon be some place else right now, Pete. Keep your nose clean."

"I'll be listening for the horses," Toronto said.

The weather didn't hold and it was snowing hard again as K, grumbling in the darkness, mounted and followed Frank Garland into the canyon of the Kenesaw. Hard going. During the first hour the column managed to make a mile. After that, they didn't.

Oglethorpe Henderson, floundering through the snow up to where Garland waited during a halt, yelled to make himself heard above the wind funneling down the canyon. "A hell of a march, Frank," he shouted. "If it gets very much worse than this we're liable not to get through."

"We'll get through," Garland told him in a grim voice and thought back to a night march that he had once been on along the Massanuttons in the Shenandoah back in sixty-four with Phil Sheridan. A long time ago. A long time. He had thought that they wouldn't get through then but they had.

They went on.

It was three in the morning and the wind, howling crazily, drove the snow in front of them as they reached the patch of timber where the Kenesaw made its bend and Garland halted them. With orders for no fires, the men huddled down in their coats to wait for the cold dawn. Toronto Peters, knowing by some sixth sense that the

167

column had come, drifted in out of the storm and he and Henderson squatted with Garland at the edge of the trees.

"It could be worse," Toronto yelled, pushing his lips close to Garland's ear so that he could be heard. "The Injuns ain't stirrin' out in this kind of weather. They don't figure that anybody else'd be crazy enough to stir out, either. An Injun's got a heap of sense sometimes, in my book."

Frank Garland ran cold fingers over his face and checked the details of his plan again in his mind. It would do, he decided. All that was left now was to wait until it got light enough for them to see where they were going —if the weather would clear a little. He put his worry about that into a question to Toronto.

"You think this storm will break soon, Pete?"

Toronto Peters considered that for a long moment, then reached a hand gingerly down to feel his leg. "Damn bullet ain't painin' now," he grunted. "Maybe it'll break, Frank."

Farther along the line of huddled men, Monk Walters sat with his back to a tree and his chin tucked into his coat while he stared off into the snow. Young Paul Fraley sat beside him. "Annie Helfron in love with you, kid?" Monk asked finally in a low voice.

Trooper Fraley stirred a little; brushed the snow from his face. "I don't know, Monk. I hope so."

"You going to marry her?"

"If she'll have me," young Fraley said slowly. "I'm not much, I guess, but we could get along."

Monk Walters thought about that for a long moment. Then he said, his voice so faint that Fraley barely heard, "You're lucky, boy. Lucky. See to it that you don't stop anything when the ball opens up a little while from now."

He lapsed into moody silence again, staring out into the falling snow. That could never work out for him and Rita, he was thinking somberly. There was too much behind them; things didn't happen so.

168

19. Battle in the Morning

DAWN BEGAN TO COME, finally. At first just an easing of the gloom through which the snow still fell—big flakes which clung to faces and hands—but the driving fury of the wind had gone now. Then the trees began to take shape around the waiting men and presently the outline of the ridge in front emerged out of the darkness. A snowy world, quiet except for the stamp of the horses held farther back in the timber and the faint mutter of men's voices.

A cold camp and a cold morning, Frank Garland was thinking as he sent Monk Walters to find Sergeant Brecheen. And a fight ahead, for Feather's braves, in those lodges down in the bowl beyond the ridge, would make that necessary. Well, that was what you drew your pay for. That was your reason for being out here.

Sergeant Brecheen came then, his thin face pinched with the cold, and squatted down in the snow while Garland drew a rough sketch for him in the growing light. "This is the ridge that's ahead of us," Garland said thinly. "The feeder canyon is here. Move to the head of it with your squad. Then stampede the pony herd—it'll spill down through the camp probably. The company will go in from the ridge as soon as it passes."

Sergeant Brecheen nodded and rubbed absently at the place where the bandage on his arm itched beneath his heavy coat. His lanky face was impassive but a certain satisfied assent glowed at the back of his eyes. It was no green, glory-hunting lieutenant who was leading them now, he was thinking. Captain Frank Garland was in command and Captain Garland knew what the score damned well was. Sergeant Brecheen liked that thought.

"Yes, sir," he said with his voice clipped as befitted a sergeant. "What about after that?"

"Come on in on the flank of the camp," Garland told him. "Clean out any braves that you find and herd the women and children inside the lodges. Any other questions?"

"No, sir," Sergeant Brecheen said and got back to his feet, dusting the snow from his knees.

"Move out, then," Garland said curtly. "See that you put that pony herd through at a run. And—good luck, sergeant."

For a moment longer Sergeant Anton Brecheen stood there in the graying light of the dawn, rubbing a hand across his chin and looking at Frank. Then he said, "We'll do that, sir. At a run. And I wish the captain good luck, too, sir."

He was gone then and Frank Garland stared after his retreating figure for a moment while awareness of his affection for these solid men of K sent a warmth through him in the chill morning. Some of them would be gone before this day's work was over—red lines drawn through names in the duty roster—but that could not be helped for that was the way that things were. The knowledge, though, could do nothing to ease a man's regrets. . . .

He shook the thought away and moved on through the snow to where Lieutenant Henderson was waiting for him with Jim Bestwood and the other two line sergeants. Squatting in the snow he motioned them around him. The light was getting better under the trees now. Sergeant Brecheen's squad was moving out, ghost riders filing through the dawn. The rest of the company was huddled in little groups, stamping feet and swinging arms to start the blood to flowing again.

"The village lies at the bottom of the bowl maybe a mile and a half beyond the ridge," Garland said now in an emotionless voice. "There are women and children in those lodges down there. We're not fighting them. So we'll go in sudden and hard and hope that the braves

170

will break for the hills when we hit them. If they do, we'll hold the camp and see what happens after that."

He fell silent for a moment, drawing little circles in the snow with his forefinger as he squatted on his heels, the others bunched tight around him. A man could be certain of nothing, he was thinking. There would be young bucks down there, already blooded and impatient for war, and if they chose to make a stand in the village it would be bad—he had no wish to hurt women and kids. Then he put the thought angrily from his mind. Damn it, you did the best you could and, if somebody got hurt, you were sorry but that was what happened when you asked for war.

"Suppose they don't break, Frank?" Henderson asked shortly.

"We've got to hope that they will." Garland's voice was tired now. "Any other questions?"

Toronto Peters came through the timber on foot then, his gimpy leg dragging a little. He had been up on the ridge and was coming back to report. Garland waited for him to speak.

"No sign of life around the camp yet," Toronto said, spitting tobacco juice into the snow. "Nothing moving except a dog or two yappin' around. Never saw nothin' so nosey as an Injun dog. You ever eat dog meat, Frank?"

Garland grinned a little, glad for the easing of the tension which the scout brought. A good man, Toronto Peters. "I never got that hungry," he said.

"Tastes a little like chicken," Toronto said thoughtfully. "Sort of like chicken that has been stewed with a skunk, I'd say. We movin' out now?"

"We're moving out," Frank Garland said, the hardness coming back into his voice again as he stood up and eased his gun belt about his hips. "Mount the company, Thorpe."

Senator Mark Hardin stood a little apart from the rest of the men, his face drawn and old. The cold bit at him despite the heaviness of the buffalo coat. It crept into his feet through the thick boots and crawled up his legs and

171

fastened itself on his stomach with tight hands. He was aware of the rough and careless talk that was going on around him in the dawn and he did not wholly understand it.

"Today you earn your pay, sonny boy," that big, red-headed corporal was saying to the trumpeter. "Today you can look Uncle right smack in the eye when you stick your hand out for the two-bits that he will pay you for climbing on top of your horse and riding over that ridge out there."

"I consider it a privilege, Mister O'Garragh," Monk Walters said in a lofty voice which carried to Mark Hardin's ears. "Does not the good Uncle do so many nice things for me?"

"Name me one," Corporal O'Garragh said sourly now.

"I could name a million," Monk Walters said flippantly as he tightened his saddle's cinch. "For one thing, every day he sees to it that I get beans and bacon and that tasty hardtack. What more could a man possibly want?"

"Cake," O'Garragh said dourly.

"Cake!" Monk repeated in a shocked voice. "Mister O'Garragh! How you do carry on!"

Why, Mark Hardin thought suddenly, *some of these men are going to be killed today! They have marched for fifty hours through the worst kind of weather. They have had no sleep and they are going to fight presently! And all this for so little—for so very little. Yet they joke about it! This is a breed of men that I have not known before.*

He thought back to the things that he had said that night as he had stood there in front of the fireplace in Major Kingman's quarters—the mouthings that he had poured on these people—and dull shame ran grayly through him so that he wanted to vomit there in the snow. What kind of a man was he? Sergeant Brecheen had come up now and was assembling his squad.

"Come on. Come on," Sergeant Brecheen was calling out in a low, crisp voice. "Get the lead out of your pants because no glory boy is leadin' us today. We're movin' out."

A voice asked, "Where to, sarge?" Brecheen laughed shortly and swung up into the saddle.

"To heaven, soldier," he said with a hard note running through his voice. "Or maybe to hell. You got any objections? Mount up! Mount up! We ain't got all day!"

Mark Hardin turned abruptly away. Somehow and all at once, he wanted to go over there to that lean, hardfaced sergeant; to tell him abjectly that he had been wrong about all this. That he hadn't understood.

But you didn't do that here. The sergeant, he knew, would look down at him with a faint tolerance in the gray dawn light. The sergeant would say, "Yes, sir," in a respectful voice. Then the sergeant would ride on off into the falling curtain of the snow and would forget all about him.

A breed of men that I have not known before, Mark Hardin thought again. *But a breed that is good!*

The group around Frank Garland broke up swiftly, men moving off through the trees to where the rest of the company waited. Low voices sung out in the eerie light and saddle leather creaked as men swung up; horses snorted uneasily as the weight of riders came onto them again. And then K marched out—ghostly riders through the snow which still fell—with Garland riding at the head of the column and Monk Walters, trumpet slung, beside him.

Fifteen minutes of marching, screened by the trees, brought them to the place that Garland had selected last night. There was a long draw here which ran parallel to the length of the hidden village, and he deployed K into a thin skirmish line with a wave of his hand. A low order passed along from mouth to mouth. Then he moved on foot with Henderson to where the gully's lip gave them a view of the snowy basin which fell away in front of them.

A mile and a half away, the lodges made silent specters in the dawn, the ends of the lodge poles reaching like black fingers into the sky. The snow thinned, then ceased to fall altogether. Nothing moved down there. No smoke curled yet in the morning air, no sound disturbed the quiet.

Garland gave the village a long scrutiny through his

field glasses, then slid them back into their case again and lay for a moment with his chin resting on his folded arms while he stared bleakly at the panorama ahead. A little wind came whirling down from the mountains to the left and lifted the snow into white swirls. A camp robber complained mournfully from the timber behind which the two men lay.

"A hell of a business, Thorpe," Frank Garland murmured under his breath. "Why should things like this be? People will die this morning. Nothing can stop that."

"I know," Oglethorpe Henderson said and fell silent again, busy with his own thoughts.

Garland went on, his voice faintly troubled. "And yet we've got no choice. If Feather isn't punished—his band broken up now—you know what will happen. Other bands will follow him off the reservation and the whole of this country will blaze again. No, we've got no choice. I don't know—maybe Feather had no choice, either."

"These things are not decided by us," Oglethorpe Henderson said soberly then. "The decision was made a long time ago, I think. When the white man first put his foot on this land, Frank. You shouldn't let this thing ride you."

"Do you think Gil Hardin is still alive?" Garland asked, abruptly changing the subject. "I am not sure that I wish he is," he added roughly and saw the faint shock which moved through Henderson's eyes.

Am I wishing that because I cannot bear the thought of Janet Davenport in his arms? he wondered angrily. *If that is so then I am worse than Gil.*

"Gil blundered," Henderson was saying with a faint reproof in his voice. "But that doesn't change the fact that Feather had already left the reservation, Frank. It doesn't bring back to life those freighters that his braves murdered, the people scalped at the stage station at Bailey's."

"I know." Garland fell silent, remembering the smoldering stage station with the mutely accusing bodies sprawled in front of it. Then he added finally, "I guess that's the way that things are."

174

A spatter of shots from across the valley jerked him out of his reverie and he said tightly now, "The ball is opening, Thorpe," and turned his body to beckon with an arm. Monk Walters came, leading the officers' horses, and Garland swung up into the saddle, lifted his arm and let it drop forward. The line of K flowed over the gully's crest at a walk, and dropped down the gentle slope and over the edge into the basin beyond.

Down below the lodges were suddenly spewing half-naked braves out into the cold dawn as Garland lifted the skirmish line into a trot. A disorganized melee of men down there milled in and out in confusion. Then a dark cloud of running horses erupted from the feeder canyon and went thundering through and around the camp to scatter onto the hills beyond.

Garland's voice carried clear and hard: "Trumpeter, sound the charge!" and Monk Walters ran his tongue over his lips and lifted the bugle to his mouth.

The brassy notes tore the morning apart, lifting the hair a little on the back of Garland's neck, and then the line of K went surging forward, horses lifted into a pounding run and men yelling as they bent low in their saddles, reins in the left hand, pistol held high in right. Snow flew from beneath the churning hoofs and the guidon snapped, crisply back in the wind.

The old, well remembered exultation possessed Frank Garland for a moment, driving away the depression which had been riding his shoulders all morning. His horse ran powerfully between his knees and the wind snapped cold against his face. This was the thing that a man was born for, he thought; this was a soldier's excuse for being. To ride at the head of a company. To savor the full, lusty zest of life for a fleeting moment. To look old fears in the eye and laugh them scornfully away.

Jim Bestwood was yelling hoarsely off to the flank, "Dress on the guidon, damn you! Dress on the guidon! Schmidt, ride that damn horse!"

The camp was close now, boiling with scurrying figures which faded swiftly back toward the rocky high ground and spewing out a heavy hail of rifle fire as they went. A bullet clipped at Garland's saddle; from the corner of his eye he saw a trooper go down—horse and man tangling in a long fall. It was Monk Walters, the trumpeter. K was firing now, powder smoke drifting darkly up through the snow which had started to fall again.

Then they were into the village and horses were plunging crazily among the lodges as troopers tried to check their headlong career. Garland shouted, his voice rasping in the morning, "Dismount and fight on foot! Make a line along the far edge of the village, Thorpe!" and the horse-holders drifted back as K yanked carbines from boots and knelt to fire at the Indians who had retreated sullenly back into the broken ground beyond the village. They moved there like dark ghosts among the rocks.

K, flung into a thin line at the edge of the village now, began a sporadic fire that sent echoes rolling back against the hills. Sergeant Brecheen came pounding in with his squad and Garland dismounted them and sent them through the camp to herd the women and children into a half-dozen lodges at the far side where they were safe from the fire. When they had done, Garland left Brecheen there to guard them and went on back to the firing line.

Oglethorpe Henderson came crawling up, his face smeared with powder smoke. He gestured roughly toward the line of rocks which lifted like a rampart a hundred yards away and slightly above the basin's floor.

"We'll have to dig them out, Frank," he said tightly. "It won't be easy. Did you find Gil?"

"No sign of him," Garland grunted. "They must have taken him with them when they pulled back. Their ace in the hole. Well, we've got an ace in the hole ourselves."

"The women and kids?"

Garland nodded. "And the camp. They're half-naked out there in the snow. I'm going forward and try to parley with them, Thorpe. Send Toronto Peters here and then cover us."

"You can't do that, Frank," Henderson said violently.

176

"It's a fool thing to chance with them jumpy from the charge and hating us the way they do!"

"It's a chance," Garland said. "I mean to take it. There's been too much killing already."

Toronto Peters came, wiping at his mustache, and Garland outlined his plan in curt, clipped words. Toronto listened, his face impassive. Then he said, "My old woman is goin' to miss me—but I'll go with you, Frank. You ain't got any corner on craziness, I guess." Garland let the tightness go out of his face for a moment.

"Hell, you'll live to be a thousand, Pete. Let's go!"

Henderson sent a command along the skirmish line and K's fire stopped and Garland, Toronto Peters following at his shoulder, stepped out into the open. He carried his right hand lifted, palm outward, in a gesture of peace. The fire from the rocks in front died away and the two men went slowly on, picking their way across the rough ground, until they stood halfway between the two lines.

"Tell Feather that I want to parley," Garland said to Toronto Peters in a low voice. "Tell him to come out and to bring the lieutenant with him if he's not afraid, Pete."

"Maybe it's my funeral oration that I'm about to give," Toronto said dourly. "Well, here goes nothin', Frank."

He began to speak, using his hands to make sign, and Garland waited with his nerves pulled tight against the expected impact of a bullet. After a moment a brave, naked in the bitter wind except for a clout and a war bonnet of eagle feathers, stood up among the rocks.

"Broken Feather," Toronto Peters grunted and then went on with his gabble. He stopped and listened as the Indian replied and then turned his head a little to Garland. "Feather says that he will listen to what you've got to say. Want me to tell him to come down here an' bring the lootenant with him, Frank?"

"Let that go for now," Garland grunted. "Say to him that it is useless for him to fight any more. Say that the soldiers will drive his braves naked back into the hills where they will freeze to death if he tries to fight. Say to

177

him that if he will surrender the braves who murdered the freighters and those people at Bailey's I will let his women and children return peaceably to the reservation. But tell him that he, himself, must come with me as a prisoner to Fort Duncan. No use trying to make this thing soft, Pete. He may as well know the worst."

"He won't do it, Frank," Toronto Peters grunted sourly. "What about Gil?"

"Tell him that he must send the lieutenant out to us now," Garland said.

Toronto Peters grunted again. "He might do that. But he won't surrender them braves to be hung an' he won't give himself up as a prisoner. It ain't in an Injun's nature."

Garland said in a harsh voice, "Tell him anyway!" and Toronto Peters let his voice go out in a long sigh and began to speak once more.

Then a voice—Gil Hardin's voice—called a high warning from up there among the rocks. "Frank! Look out, Frank!"

The voice died chokingly away as a blunt fist suddenly slammed into Frank Garland's chest, chopping off the strength of his knees and sending a long shudder rippling through the length of him. As he crumpled forward, he heard the slam of a single shot echo from the hillside and then everything was strangely quiet.

He knew vaguely that men were yelling from the direction of the camp; that men were going by on either side of him with their bodies bent forward and their mouths open and their carbines slamming fire ahead of them as they ran. It was K going in, he thought with a dreamy aloofness.

A good company. A good company. . . .

178

20. So a Man's Luck Must Run

IT WAS EARLY AFTERNOON when consciousness seeped slowly back into his mind like the slow pulling apart of dark curtains which had closed off the world. He was lying in one of the lodges—the rank, smoky smell told him that —as memory of the morning began to come back, a flash here, a hazy glimpse there dimly seen.

The line of K pouring down over the basin's lips. Trooper Walters going down with his horse. Broken Feather standing sullenly there with the snow and the dark firs behind him. Gil Hardin's voice lifting in that choked yell.

It was dim in here in the lodge and he rolled his head a little and saw that a man was squatted there by his side. It was young Fraley, he saw, and his thoughts wandered back to the yellow-haired girl who had stood at the gate at Fort Duncan as the column had ridden out. That had been a long time ago, he thought vaguely. A long time ago.

Then he knew that pain was a burning iron in his side and that his mouth was dry with a harsh dryness which was bitter and tasted bad. Voices came from beyond the lodge's opening and he could see through enough to tell that the snow was still falling. Time to be moving on—moving on.

"Where am I hit?" he asked aloud then and was a little surprised to find that he could speak. He saw young Fraley's worried face bending over him.

"In the belly, sir," Fraley said, his voice scared. "You hadn't ought to try to talk, I don't think."

"Is Lieutenant Henderson still alive?"

"Yes, sir."

"Get him," Garland whispered.

179

Oglethorpe Henderson came after a little; dropped down on one knee and showed Garland a face which was drawn and tired. "How do you feel, Frank?" he asked slowly.

"All right," Garland said, trying to push his voice back into its old habit of command. Then he swore at the pain which came suddenly to thrust a knife through his body. "What happened?"

"Feather is dead. Twelve of his braves. That many more wounded. K went in hard after they dropped you."

"How about K, Thorpe?"

"Walters, Schmidt, Sergeant Unmack dead," Henderson said wearily. "Four wounded besides you. Not too bad —they can still ride, I think. The rest of Feather's braves have scattered for the hills and we've got the women and children. If we take them back to Duncan, the braves will come drifting in after a while. I think that we've broken the back of this thing, Frank."

Again remembrance of that voice which had called out the warning to him came back to Garland. "Gil?" he asked.

"Dead, too." Henderson's voice was flat, steady. "They jumped him after he tried to warn you. He put up a good fight before they downed him, Frank. Too many for him, though. He was dead when we got there."

"Too bad," Garland whispered. "Too bad."

Henderson lifted a hand and passed it tiredly across his face; looked beyond Frank at the falling snow. "I guess that sort of washes out that other business, Frank."

"I guess it does," Garland said, his voice little more than a whisper. The light of the lodge's opening was trying to slip away from him again, becoming fuzzy and more gray. "What about his father, Thorpe?"

Mark Hardin's voice came from the shadows at the far side of the lodge, the voice of an old and broken man. A voice faintly pleading. Frank Garland listened to it with a vague detachment, as though he stood far to one side and watched impersonally the things that were going on elsewhere. Things that no longer concerned him now—that were the affair of others.

180

"He died like a soldier," Mark Hardin was saying. "Like that young trumpeter and the sergeant on the hillside. During the years that are left to me, I can remember that and be proud. For there are many things that I shall have to live with, Captain Garland, and there will be only one in which there is pride."

Frank Garland didn't try to answer; there was no answer to be made. The outlines of Oglethorpe Henderson's face were beginning to shimmer crazily and the pain had become a live thing which surged and ebbed, surged and ebbed.

Toronto Peters came into the lodge, easing his spare frame through the opening. "How is he?" he asked. Henderson shook his head.

"Pretty bad," he said somberly. "Not likely that he'll last until we can get him back to Duncan, Pete. Why did it have to be him?"

"It's always the good ones," Toronto Peters said. "He's tough, though. You'll ride with him again, one of these days, lieutenant."

Garland heard that as from a great distance; he didn't care very much. The dark curtains were being pulled slowly shut around him again and he began to drift away, rising and falling as though that wind which had blown down the canyon of the Kenesaw had picked him up now and was bearing him away on its wings.

Trooper Otto Fleigheimer, a bandage about his head, sat on a rock in the snow and stared bleakly off at the hills which lifted their white slopes into the dying afternoon. From where he sat he could see the three still shapes, each covered by its blanket, which lay between two of the lodges. Trooper Schmidt there and Sergeant Unmack. And Monk Walters, Trooper Fleigheimer thought dully. He rubbed his big, red hands together with a nervous gesture and looked at them and then put them into the pockets of his coat.

And Monk Walters. He felt stunned every time that he thought of that. Lonesome and cheated somehow.

Corporal O'Garragh came slowly by in the snow, glanced at Fleigheimer with no expression on his face. Then he squatted on his heels while he reached for tobacco and papers. He made his cigarette, taking his time and smoothing the paper with careful fingers and then smoked, neither man saying anything for a long moment as the day began to fade.

Finally, Corporal O'Garragh threw away the last of his cigarette and stood up. "He was a good little man," he said soberly. "A good little man, Fleigheimer."

Trooper Fleigheimer nodded mutely. He wanted to say something; to say that Monk Walters had given him the comfort of assurance when he had been afraid. To say that Monk Walters had been the one who had kept him from going over the hill on that night before K had marched out of Fort Duncan. But those words wouldn't come.

"I thought I was the one that was going to get it," he managed in a low voice at last. "It would have been better if it had been that way."

Corporal O'Garragh gave him a long look—a look which was different from his usual impatient regard. "You're all right, Otto," he said then and went on off toward the picket line, kicking the snow angrily as he went.

Dreams bothered Frank Garland.

There was that tortured ride back to Fort Duncan, slung in a blanket between two led horses and long snatches of that pushed into his dreams. And there was the memory of Duncan's main gate as they had passed slowly through while faces watched from either side. Those faces kept floating in his dreams but they seemed somehow to be the faces of strangers. Disembodied and impersonal and meaning nothing to him now.

And later there were voices but they were vague and indistinct and he had no interest in what they were saying. And then there was the pain, burning in his side with red waves which flooded and ebbed. Flooded and ebbed.

The world had become a long, dim corridor down which he wandered, searching for a door but the door eluded him—seemed always to be just ahead. Heat came to make a solid wall around him and he pushed his way into it, angry that he could not break through it and leave it behind. Then, for the space of an eternity, the heat would go away and leave him shivering miserably in the grip of an icy wind which whistled out of nowhere and blew its chill breath against him and then went stomping away again.

He climbed an iron ladder which was let into a cliff—up and up until he was lost in the clouds and great, black birds came to fly about his head and make mournful cawing noises. One perched on his shoulder and he beat at it with a hand, for the bird's weight was pressing him down so that he couldn't climb. The birds went away, their sad cries coming faintly back to him and he was in the Shenandoah again, marching at night along the Massanuttons with Phil Sheridan and a man was calling to him from somewhere.

It was on the third day after they had brought him back to the hospital at Fort Duncan that the shadows began to thin a little and awareness come back into him and he could hear voices speaking and they made sense. He lay still with his eyes closed and listened, faintly puzzled. There were fingers on his wrist and one of the voices—that would be Doc Smedley, the contract surgeon—was saying the same thing that Toronto Peters had said back there in the snowy basin beside the Kenesaw. A long time ago, Frank Garland thought and was surprised at the clarity of his perceptions.

"The fever has broken, Miss Davenport." Yes, that was Doc Weeks, all right. "He's a tough man. A very tough man. Anybody else would be dead by now, I think. But, with good nursing, he ought to pull through."

A woman's voice said softly, "He'll have good nursing, Captain Weeks," Garland knew that it was Janet there beside his bed. It made him feel good—damned good—and he lay still, keeping his eyes closed and hoping that she'd speak again.

The doctor was going on in his dry, professional voice. "He'll sleep naturally tonight and that is the best medicine for him now. He should mend quickly with the fever gone. Are you going my way, Lieutenant Henderson?"

Thorpe's voice, hearty and glad, answered. "As far as the Kingmans', doc. I want to stop in and see the major for a minute. I guess it will be 'Colonel Kingman' any day now, though. You know about that, don't you?"

"I have heard the rumor," the doctor said.

"No rumor," Oglethorpe Henderson told him and Frank Garland, listening alertly now, heard the deep satisfaction in his lieutenant's voice. "Senator Hardin promised that before he left for Washington. Promised that Caleb Kingman would remain here in command of Fort Duncan for as long as he wished."

That was good, Garland thought. Yes, good.

"It's a pity," the contract surgeon was saying, "that a man must lose a son, lieutenant, in order that his eyes may be finally opened. I will see you tomorrow, Miss Davenport. Don't stay with him too long tonight. The sleep that he gets now is the best drug that I've got in my bag."

Janet said, "Yes, doctor," in a soft voice, and then Garland heard footsteps receding across the floor and the sound of a door closing. He opened his eyes and saw Janet there with the lamplight bright across her face. "Janet," he whispered, and she smiled tenderly down at him and then bent slowly to kiss him on the lips. A kiss with a vast sweetness in it.

"I am so glad, my darling," she said.

"I dreamed of you," he whispered, his voice husky. "I've dreamed of you since I first saw you on the train."

"You mustn't try to talk now, Frank," she said, placing gentle fingers on his lips. "There will be plenty of time for talk later. Years and years of time, my very dear."

And Frank Garland knew that that was so and gladness ran through him. He smiled, contented, as he drifted into a sleep which was easy and dreamless now.

It was the sound of Tattoo which awakened him later. The lights were out and Janet had gone and there was nothing but the pungent smells and the quiet sounds of the hospital around him. He lay, staring into the darkness and listening to bugle's silvery song as the long notes drifted in to him through the window. And thoughts marched through his mind with a steady cadence.

Thoughts which had troubled him for a long time now but which seemed to have resolved themselves here in this darkened room. Pictures which made up the pattern of his living.

Janet and the promise that he had seen in her clear eyes and that was a thing very precious. Major Caleb Kingman and the patient courage in his face and in the face of Marjory standing proudly beside him. And that was good. Company K swinging across the basin's snowy lip. Jim Bestwood and Tim O'Garragh and young Paul Melrose Fraley and the three who had died back there beside the Kenesaw. All of those things.

And the answer to all that had bothered him came now to stand with him beside the bed in which he lay. The answer to all of the doubts and all of the half-fears.

For a man did not serve for himself or by himself, he thought. A man served that he might stand—with a deep pride running in him—beside all of these others. These solid people who had come here, forsaking lesser things, so that they might hold their heads high and say, "We are the Army!"

"We are the ones who carry the flag out here in the van. We are the ones who keep the faith."

And Frank Garland knew now that it was good to stand with them. It would be good through all of the years still to come for Janet would be beside him.

In the sutler's store, Corporal Greenbriar from headquarters smoked his cigar and looked at Trooper Otto Fleigheimer with ill-disguised disdain. There had been many reports to make out concerning the expedition to the Kenesaw and it had meant extra work for Corporal Greenbriar and he was in a bad humor.

"I thought that you were the joker that was going to get

out of the Army and go to St. Louis," he said unpleasantly. "Or New York or wherever it was."

"What of it?" Fleigheimer grunted.

The irritation increased in the corporal's face. "So now you've changed your mind and are going to sign up for another hitch," he said. "Well, well, well. I'd have thought that you'd got your bellyful of the Army up there on the Kenesaw."

Fleigheimer looked at the other out of the corners of his eyes—he didn't like Corporal Greenbriar. "I'm re-enlisting," he said heavily. "You want to make something of that?"

Greenbriar yawned widely and his ill-humor increased as he stared back. "It's your funeral," he said. "We'll pat you into place with a spade one of these days. Like we did that trumpeter in——"

Otto Fleigheimer said violently then, "You keep Trumpeter Monk Walters' name out of that filthy mouth of yours!" and slugged Corporal Greenbriar squarely between the eyes with a big fist and went on out and into the night.

Corporal O'Garragh was there and together the two of them walked slowly back to K's barracks. By the main guardhouse, L Company's trumpeter moistened his lips and, after a moment, the long and silvery notes of Tattoo drifted across the parade ground. Lifting and falling and dying away into the shadows and neither man spoke until it was done.

Corporal O'Garragh said then, "Monk used to blow it better," and Fleigheimer nodded and they went on.

ABOUT WILLIAM CHAMBERLAIN

William Chamberlain, who is carried on the rolls of the Department of Defense as Brigadier General Edwin W. Chamberlain, USAF, Retired, has been writing stories about soldiers for upwards of twenty years. About TRUMPETS OF COMPANY K he writes:

"This is the story of one of those little expeditions which were legion among our Regular Army during the period between the close of the Civil War and the turn of the century. Each, in itself, is of little importance or significance—except to the men who died therein—but taken *in toto* these unsung and obscure actions achieve the status of a major conflict in importance, for it was by these tiny successes that the West was won.

"The men who died in Company K had no knowledge that they were dying to achieve a national goal and, had they had such knowledge, they would not have cared. For the most part, they were simple people. Professional soldiers. In a word, the Regular Army. In this book I have tried to put down the things that made up, in part at least, their lives. Something of what they thought and felt and did. For they were the forgotten men of that time. A great war had shortly ended and the country was tired of soldiers and impatient with soldiering. Most of its people neither knew nor cared about that scant handful of men who, for beans and bacon and small pay, were making possible the development of the West. Yet those old professionals in blue trousers—usually reinforced with white canvas at knee and seat —were the sentinels keeping the peace while America grew."

General Chamberlain was born at Challis, Idaho, in 1903. He graduated from West Point in 1927, from where he went to the Philippine Islands as a second lieutenant of Coast Artillery, later transferring successively to the Infantry and the Air Force. In 1940 he was made a member of the War Department General Staff, in which capacity he served until his retirement for physical disability, with the rank of brigadier general, in 1946. During World War II he was in all of the major overseas theaters and was awarded the Distinguished Service Medal.

In 1928 he was married to Marian Corbett, herself the daughter of an army officer, in the Philippine Islands. She is, of course, the "Army Wife" to whom the book is dedicated. They have two sons; a third son was killed in action in Korea. At present they make their home in Coral Gables, Florida.

This is General Chamberlain's first book-length work. His stories appear frequently in most of the national magazines, including *The Saturday Evening Post.*

Ride into the world of adventure with Ballantine's western novels!